Seasons

Book Three
of
The Tripper Series

by

C.M. Halstead

To Those That Believe

One

For Grey, time-travel became a commute a long time ago. Perhaps he should consider retirement or that training gig Colonel Petzer pitched to him.

Slowly at first, the room's papers and dust fly about. The paper rises effortlessly, and it hovers in place ever so slightly before the increasing current makes it take flight. The heavier dust starts to swirl in its own vortex on the surface of the room, its circle widening, and then taking off. The dust first creates a mini tornado and then breaks up as the air movement becomes more forceful and random.

Lights whisper, breaking the room's darkness ever so slightly, increasing their presence in-sync with the air movement. Random colors appear, blinking red, orange, green, all the colors of the rainbow and then some, appear from thin air as the large back wall of the room becomes opaque and swirls from a point in its center about 1/3 the height of the wall. A wormhole manifests from the wall.

Seven human figures appear in the hazy dust-filled light. Thrust into the large room with a gigantic invisible force; it takes milliseconds to move the figures from the wormhole and deposit them in a reverse bowling pin pattern in the landing area. The humans are oblivious. Even their clothing was impervious to the movement.

In a kneeling position, Grey has an eye on each of his team members as soon as he is cognizant the tram-ride is over. Well, almost over. The electricity that the journey overwhelms him with still pulses through his body. He knows he cannot stand up until the feeling has left him, but he can look over his team to make sure they all made it and are still breathing.

All six are in place in front of him, none the worse for wear from their double trip back in time, all the way to 1917. On their short layover in 2014, Rosa examined June, other than some severe bruises; she is no worse for wear. Even her mental state is strong and healthy. Grey had informed her that if she wants, she can report to the medical center upon their return, and they will make all the pain go away and the gigantic ugly bruises as well.

Grey himself has a few bruises from his interaction with the drunken sailors. None worth treating in his mind, he long ago got used to body pain caused by wear and tear. He will only go to the medical center if something is broken and in need of fixing.

As he feels the electric force leaving his body, Miokel falling to the ground in front of him catches his eye. Grey wills himself to stand up. He moves to where Miokel is lying on the ground and, with purpose, kneels next to him. He pulls his mini AED from its' pouch and places two fingers onto Miokel's neck in the back corner by his jawbone, feeling for a pulse he is certain will not be there. It is not.

Charles appears, his AED ready, with electrodes in his hands, one each. He places one over the heart area of Miokel's chest and the other off to the opposite side of his rib cage. Charles watches Grey's face.

"No pulse, zap him," Grey says, removing his fingers from Miokel's neck.

Charles pushes the button not once but twice. Miokel arches slightly off the floor. The modern version of the AED uses smart technology, therefore not needing to be as powerful as the ones of the 20th century. The electric charge sent into Miokel's body seeks out the heart; it wants the heart, thrives off the connection with it. The two separate charges make a bee-line for each other in the chest cavity and collide instantly in the heart, startling it awake. The second charge arriving a second later, not needed, is instead absorbed to assist the heart in getting the electrical system of Miokel's body moving again.

Miokel opens his eyes as if from a nightmare. They look startled and deadly at the two men looking down at him.

"Damn." is the first word out of Miokel's mouth.

Charles and Grey smile, both knowing what the word is about. They help him into a sitting position as his body returns to functioning.

Although not fully cognizant yet, Miokel knows what happened; he had his first death experience as a Tripper. There goes his record! He had the un-official longest streak in Tripper history, the Trippers have been told the higher-ups don't want them to keep track of things like this, but being of the field mentality, the Trippers do it anyway. The knowledge passes through the teams slow since the only interactions between them are from Trippers, who are former teammates, now on different teams running into each other in the halls of the underground facility. It is during their catch-up conversations that these things get passed from team to team.

Charles speaks first, "So much for increasingly longest streak in the history of tripperville. Now let's see how long it takes the rest of us to catch up to you."

Miokel flashes a grimace, instead of the joyful smile he intended. He reaches for Charles, they embrace forearms, and Charles pulls as they grip each other's muscles and squeeze, assisting Miokel to his feet. Charles steadies him for a moment, then lets go.

The rest of the team is on their feet, and their mood lightens as soon as they see Miokel stand.

Grey, however, is still kneeling, lost in thought. John walks up to him and puts out his hand, wanting to provide an assist.

Grey stays lost in thought until John taps him, a hand on the shoulder. He offers his hand again, "May I?"

Grey stands immediately and says, "No, thank you. It wasn't that."

"Then what is it?" John, always one to ask any question to anybody.

Grey twists his mouth into the shape of someone who is perplexed, "This is the second mission in a row one of our AEDs failed. Once every ten maybe, but twice in a row? I'm going to talk with those techs!" he says.

"Let me do it, boss." John says.

Grey gives him a contemplative look.

"You know they are my people," John adds, smiling.

A couple of team members laugh, knowing he speaks the truth. Not only does Grey think John is ready to take action on things like this, he is grateful to have someone like John to talk to these tech geeks. He doesn't quite speak their language, and the ballsier ones seem to enjoy spinning words into a way that Grey doesn't understand them, yet the other technicians standing around are always nodding their heads in agreement. At least that is what Grey's ego tells him. He believes most are smart enough not to mess with the likes of him, or is that another consolation belief from his ego?

"Great, handle it, and report back to me asap." Grey looks around, wanting to confirm the bag of rocks or jewels, whatever they are, are not still with the team. The PABs have a tendency to grab whatever objects are important to them; he just didn't want to leave them lying there on the floor.

A distant voice echoes down on them from above, "Everything ok down there?" It is Loren, and he is standing on the landing outside the control room. They can watch the travel area from above through a giant window.

The landing he is standing on was installed when the route to the machine was altered awhile back. Wanting a way to communicate if necessary, without taking the long walk all the way around, or without the necessity of giving emergency personnel clearance to enter the top-secret area of the machine. The fewer people that have permission to pass through the booby-trapped entrance, the better.

Though, one would think that a long rope tied to the landing would allow security free access to the machine. That person would be thinking without a strong knowledge of the type of organization they are dealing with. There is sure to be some sort of unseen death-causing protection between Lauren's position and the floor.

Grey gives him two thumbs up.

"Ok, let us get out of here, "Grey says to his team.

The giant orbital sander that is the machine is ending its desire to move the paper and dust through the air, and it comes to a rumbling halt. The last of the dirt, once again losing to the law of gravity, falls straight to the floor while a few errant pieces of paper weave a path on self-created currents, are on a slower descent to the surface of the room.

Having gathered their wits, the team files over to the stairs and descends them, walks towards and then through the double doors that absentmindedly guard the entrance to the machine's foyer. The teams walk through the high-tech, low-tech defenses of the space between sets of swinging doors. There is something brilliant about combining bio-readers and trap doors.

The Trippers exit the far set of doors, entering the hallway that takes them to the main facility.

Their pace quickens as their bodies subconsciously long for the food they know is waiting for them in their ready-room.

"Are you joining us this time?" Rosa asks Grey, remembering he had to go see the new boss immediately after their last mission. "Yes, he has given me permission to debrief after we eat. He now knows our routines and the importance of eating together post-mission. Perhaps it was him having to listen to my belly the last time that encouraged his decision." Grey laughs at his joke.

Rosa pats him affectionately with her fist and says, "Awesome, just awesome, and I won't have to make anybody wait this time. We went ahead and ate last time as you directed, but this time I was planning on aborting that order and making us all wait. Of course, I was going to tell you ahead of time to guilt you into hurrying through your meeting!"

She smiles at him.

Grey smiles and nods. He is grateful as well, for his stomach did talk through the entire meeting with his new boss, although they both had ignored it the whole time.

Two

The team sits, consuming their victory meal, wallowing in their safe return. After only a few mouthfuls, John cannot help himself.

"So, Charles, how did you learn the whole spike through the glass magic trick?"

"I came across the right materials, then made the spikes out of them, and practiced a lot. Like, too much, until one day, I was consistent. I have carried them ever since.

"I did not want to carry them until I mastered it. Especially since I had read about it in a book and had never seen it done. No way I would take it to work until I knew it would not fail me when I needed it most."

"Teach me." John requests.

"Find your spikes, and I will." Charles responds.

Grey finishes cleaning his plate with a piece of bread; after popping the bread into his mouth, he looks around the table, searching the mood. Most are in a balanced place, June seems out of sorts.

"How yah doing down there, June?" He asks of her.

June puts on her best smile and says, "Fine."

"Utoh." A few team members say in unison.

June smiles in response." I am fine. I am sore is all."

"One trip to the medical center can heal all if you choose." Grey responds.

"No, thank you. I will take the reminder. Humans can be cruel and I forget. I want the reminder that I was cruel."

"You aren't cruel." Mackenzie blurts.

Looking at Mackenzie, Grey says, "It seems June is dealing with a guilty conscience."

Mackenzie scoffs, "Why, what is bad about what we just accomplished? We set someone free who really deserved to be free and helped capture an evil dude. Seems legit to me."

June's eyes well up, the spring ready to flow.

Grey speaks, "I don't think that is it, Mac."

Charles' turn, "Medical Center can help with a guilty conscience too. They have paid listeners." He says with a smile.

For now, it seems June is content on devouring her Chicago style pizza. She eats with vigor, devouring carbs and fat, the comfort settling in.

Rosa lets out a soft burp, it softly escapes the hand over

her mouth. Eliciting a chuckle from Miokel, who takes the opportunity to ask his need to know before I die question.

"So, Grey, what do you do with a drunken sailor?" He asks with a smirk on his face and gratuitous eye contact.

Grey guffaws, a gratuitous raucous sound, bounces around the ready room. The team is in good spirits, another successful mission, this time, no-one died from their hands at least.

Instead of answering the question, Grey pushes back his chair and, with his hands on the table, says, "You have the next five days. As a reminder to the rookies, rest, don't exert yourself too much. The body needs rest. Whatever builds you up, June. Focus on that for the duration. Other than that, I will see you at 9am on our Monday. Above all, have fun."

Grey gets up and removes himself from the room. Ready to get his debriefing with Colonel Petzer over so he can get showered and lost in his virtual reality system.

Three

Rosa lounges on a giant U-shaped couch while she reads her book, plush and full of pillows, she has created a perfect reading nest. Spending a majority of her downtime in it, reading whatever she can get her hands on, she alternates between reading and everything else. Everything else being: gratuitous exercise, food, and the occasional bath. She often reads while doing those things also.

Rosa is not selective when it comes to her reading medium. She prefers paper books whenever possible, although her tablet providing about 1000 books to choose from, makes it her preferred choice for reading long series of books. The ability to track multiple books with a flip of her wrist is a luxury she enjoys in her current life.

In her younger days, when the Marine Corps relocated her, she was forced to choose between selling, giving away or keeping, a bulk of the books she acquired while at each station. Back in her day, she wasn't technically allowed to work combat zones, so she always had the luxury of a room with a spot for a shelf or two. She sometimes acquired a spare footlocker and filled it to the brim with books as well. Once she got used to the lifestyle, she gained satisfaction in moving said footlocker out into a staging area for Marines. She would stand there to protect it from an ornery Staff Sergeant or a young punk second lieutenant wanting to prove his worth.

She would encourage the Marines preparing to ship out or returning from deployment to grab some reading material for their rucksacks and seabags. She was always pleasantly surprised at the number of Marines taking her up on the free books and just as enamored with the ones who would remove finished ones from their gear and deposit them in the footlocker after choosing a new one to take to war with them. When she was out of time, she might pick through the remnants for unread material for herself and then take the remainder to a library or some type of donation area. Other times she happily picked up an empty footlocker and went about her business.

She remembers being elated about the empty footlocker, content to distribute this type of knowledge, as opposed to the kind of data, knowledge, and information she dealt with during the work hours.

That information was used to send Marines to combat or for political gain, she is sure...not quite as empowering as helping her fellow Marines escape their grind for a bit. That story or book enables them to experience something other than blood, death, and chaos, at least that is what the storyteller in her brain tells her.

Rosa stretches her arm out above her, feeling the need to put the book down, she enters a full-body stretch. Having spent most of the last couple of days on the couch, her body has tightened up a bit. Knowing she has a few hours before her scheduled departure time with Charles and John, she lays out her perfect get ready plan: an hour of stretching and ti chi, a long bath, and then dress comfortably to hang out with the guys. Rosa learned long ago that looking good and being uncomfortable is not necessarily related.

She knows she can dress just about any way she wants and will still be able to pick up whomever in the city; she is a bit of an exotic while in Namazinga-2.

Located in North America's southwest area, there are more people of Irish and Latino heritage than her pure Spanish heritage. That, combined with her higher than average confidence, and knowledge that any woman can find their way into sex anywhere, at any time, she dresses the way she wants to.

The utilitarian style clothing of Namazinga-2 suits her just fine.

Her stretch complete; she picks her book up again and gets lost in it for a while longer.

Her apartment around her, free of distractions and decorated with military sparseness, is also free of clutter and dust. She pays someone to come and clean it once a week. Forget doing it herself. Reading is way more important. More important than just about anything on her days off.

Only one wall of her apartment holds more than one item; on this wall is a grouping of plaques. When she was recruited years ago, she happened to be carrying the contents of the office she had just left. Formerly her office, it now belonged to the new captain of the S.W.A.T. team, she having been let go and kicked out of the police force for something, to this day, she would attest she didn't do. Although it is not something she justifies talking about, she will look anyone in the eye and say she was framed for something she did not do, and she knows who framed her. Unfortunately, he was too powerful and untouchable for the law to do anything about the injustice. She was formulating a plan to end him herself just for honor reasons, when she was forced into a van, office-in-a-box and all.

Thinking for sure she had been abducted by the man who set her up, she was relieved (once she stopped fighting that is) to learn that they were not who she thought they were, and perplexed as hell when they gave her their pitch. She remembers laughing and calling them all sorts of creative things before they presented her with proof that the story they were spinning was not a tale. The rest is history as they say. Rosa knows this third title she earned will be her last. First the title of US Marine, then SWAT, and now a Tripper, three hefty titles indeed.

Sinking back into her book, Rosa sets her mental alarm clock for 30 minutes; it will rouse her when it is time to get ready for town. She smirks a bit, knowing that going to Namazinga-2 with John will be entertaining!

Four

Namazinga

(na-MAZIN-ga)

The high-speed train reaches the enclosed city; used to high-speed transportation, Colonel Petzer is unfazed by the process. Stoic, he disembarks himself into a nondescript space between the VIP area and the entrance to the lower city.

Unnoticed in the shadows, he walks towards a wide blank section of the wall. As he approaches, part of it silently moves to the side, leaving a three by seven-foot space for the Colonel to walk through. He does.

The sliding door closes behind him and then the internal lights turn on. No shadows emitted to enlighten any to its existence. The space between the walls is unknown to most. Those graced with logic, and the confidence to use it, must know hidden areas of the city exists. They do in every city.

Wherever there are humans, there is waste and it must go somewhere. Anywhere there are lights, there is electricity and those lines must run somewhere. Anywhere there is water, the clean and dirty water must flow somewhere. This is not that somewhere.

Colonel Petzer walks the space alone, the floor and walls of the area absorb his steps by design, none of the usual sounds exist. Just the ones in his brain.

Colonel Petzer loves the silence. At first, it is deafening. The Tinnitus in his ears usually roars for attention at first, then calms down after a few moments. Used to hum's from machinery, the sounds of air flowing and contained humans, the Colonel thrives in the secret passages' sound vacuum. One, who moves typically at a fast pace, he actually slows down here. His brain does the same; it gets away from its frantic content and focuses in the quiet. This is why he stops walking about ten feet before the elevator's sensor; he knows once he engages that, the doors will open, and his sensory deprivation time is over until he leaves the city again.

Pausing to focus on the quiet, Colonel Petzer swears he

can hear the soft drum on the city's beat through the walls...perhaps it is ghost memories in his ears. Sometimes when he stops to listen, all he hears is complete silence; other days, like today, his brain screams venomously and allows him no peace.

He takes a step forward and the doors come open. The guard inside nods his recognition. "Good to see you, sir." he says.

The Colonel smiles. He recognizes him; also, the trooper's nickname fits to a tee. "Sgt. Bruno, glad you are still kicking and have reached retirement." he says back to the old trooper. This is an inside joke to all that have served in the special forces under Colonel Petzer; living to the age of retirement is no small feat. These young men and women who do still have a multitude of years in their bodies, albeit several bouts of post-traumatic stress lie dormant in their future, whether they like it or not—impending doom for a 28-year-old human.

"Bored to death yet?" the Colonel asks him.

"Absolutely, sir. Going from mixing it up regularly to standing in an elevator waiting for the likes of you- no offense, Colonel, is boring as hell. It will take a while to move on from hyper-vigilance mode."

The elevator, only having 30 yards to travel, arrives at its destination and the doors open.

"If ever, Sgt. Bruno, if ever." Colonel Petzer says as he

puts out his hand. Sgt. Bruno, with no hesitation, shakes it in return. He's been waiting years to shake the Colonel's hand. The only true feeling of special forces retirement, before that it is hand salutes and orders only.

Colonel Petzer makes eye contact with his former trooper and sees the guilt and shame deep in the eyes. Knowing the sergeant will have to face this soon, he roots for him. The other side of that piece of work is incredible.

Stepping out of the elevator, the Colonel enters the top half of Namazinga-2 city life. Still in the shadows until he steps through a hedgerow, he wastes no time stepping through.

Gaudier than the lower floors, it takes a moment to readjust. His time living in an underground concrete complex has not helped to squelch the surreal feeling of entering this part of a city. Again, to beat something in, he has a life of military service and special forces, the antithesis of, but a requirement for this type of life to exist.

As Colonel Petzer pauses and looks around, he realizes gaudy isn't the right word. Strangely perfect is the phrase that comes to his mind, in this moment, he desires to be a stronger wordsmith. There aren't military words to describe what he is seeing. None of the traditional acronyms apply, they being definitions of bad situations. When he looks around, he sees a perfect blend of buildings and landscapes. Although the trees, plants, and flowers acquired by his vision are planted and maintained by human beings, they appear naturally located and in perfect harmony with the walkways and broadways. Having traveled to a few of the modern cities, he already knows it is current culture to utilize natural materials gathered from the local areas outside the cities. One of the things his troops were utilized for was protecting the workers who left the city to gather said materials. Although construction on most of these cities was completed about 2100 AD, they have reached a stage where repairs are necessary, as is true with anything, they must be maintained to exist through time.

From time-to-time, these collection groups were brazenly attacked by raiding parties. Although none of the workers are sheep and are capable of wielding objects to defend themselves, it is a great idea to have professionals along, who, trained in tactics and procedures, entice these raiding parties to disappear sooner than later. For all their intention is to disrupt and create an awareness to their version of the cause, they do not have the human numbers or military-type equipment to stand up to the entire system. Instead, they thrive on guerrilla type tactics.

Not surprised he is daydreaming about confrontations, Colonel Petzer skips the opportunity to give himself a hard time about it and instead starts walking. He strolls at a military pace, other people stroll at an unhurried pace, talking and bantering with each other as they make their way to, well wherever they are going. In this part of every city, schedules are a minimum and a rarity. He knows from experience that gatherings are scheduled for "Tuesday afternoon" or "sunset on Friday," that sort of thing. Those that thrive on schedules tend to live below, or are encouraged to relax their scheduling. Since time-pieces are considered cliche and uncouth, they are unavailable except through the black market of goods flowing back and forth between the city layers.

Encouraged by the local culture, he slows his walking pace a little. At least enough to allow himself to look up at the two to four-story structures around him, a few more stories above is the top structure of the city. The buildings themselves are unique arrangements of red sandstone, yellow sandstone, limestone, and basalt rock, some of it presented in their natural forms. Patterns of the rocks and arrangement methods create artful finishes to the structures. The structures themselves are created by grinding and blending the stones with materials that concrete them together. Some are red sandstone, others a sun-bleached yellow, while others are the natural limestone's signature white. The grey basalt rock, not known to grind to powder and consisting of a dark grey, is reserved for structural finish and ambiance in its contrast to the subtlety of the other three colors. The natural hues of the buildings blend and accentuate the greens of the trees, the multitude of colors from the flowers are an expansive accompaniment.

There is a part of Colonel Petzer that walks lighter and feels at peace when he walks the walkways of this city. By design in his conscious brain, he is still unaware of its effects until it is perceived. Even his busy, blinders off, battle-stained mind succumbs to it. And he loves it.

As he reaches his destination, a sink of dread enters his belly; it always does when he enters this building. Dealing with politicians does that to him. Colonel Petzer doesn't necessarily believe them to be bad, just a different type of human whom thinks entirely different from him; popularity and chameleon promises aren't something he utilizes to get his way. These men and women hardly get their hands dirty; instead, they employ others to do so. These others, glad in their jobs, ensure their politicians work their way into power, adjust perspective of rival politicians, as well as eliminate threats to their rise in power.

After the utopian-like walk from the elevator to this building's steps, his mind reminds him, this utopia is in constant threat from those that do not understand it.

Colonel Petzer increases his pace as he takes the flagstone stairs one at a time, built large it would be hard to take them two at a time and he settles for twice the pace of others around him. Nodding his head hello to a couple groups of people sitting and talking on the steps, he generally keeps his vision focused on the impeccable double doors at the back of the top landing.

The two doors are made of local Ponderosa pine. Most of the building entries are constructed from two gigantic 200-year-old specimens, growing long and tall like the ones towering above the entrance to the underground facility; it is no stretch that they would provide enough wood if utilized correctly. Above the two doors, engraved into the sandstone, is an old symbol of justice with the words, "To protect us from Ourselves." adorned above. The Colonel smiles every time he reads the words because he knows it is true. Half the smile is for the blindfold on the lady holding the scales of justice. The established systems through time are blind; it is the human in them that slue the scale-up and down.

Entering the building, he nods to a few acquaintances as he takes the set of stairs to the right of the door. Up to the third floor, he goes to will grab a bite to eat with some friends before heading to his meeting. Knowing that he is expected to arrive "this afternoon," he has plenty of time for chow and a catch-up.

Colonel Petzer walks the hall almost to the end and enters the open door on his right. A female guard and a man behind a desk are flirting with each other. She while standing at her post, he while sitting at his. The seated man glances at Colonel Petzer, then back at the object of his flirtation just in time to see her stiffen to full attention. Disappointment crosses his face involuntarily. He stands and welcomes this Colonel he has seen many times before.

"Welcome, sir. I will inform the Chancellor of your arrival."

Thank you." Colonel Petzer replies as the gatekeeper heads for a set of closed double doors. He glances over at the guard, standing tall at her post.

"At ease, you were doing nothing but standing at your post and being human." He says.

"Thank you, sir." She relaxes her stance enough to breathe. In her mind, a legend just walked into the room. She had no idea he is in this city, nor would she have had cause to know. She does know he is the one that created and ran the most infamous group of troopers ever! When he retired, his legendary stories ran rampant through the corps. He was a propagandists dream, and many in the regular corps tried out for his program because of its reputation for weeding out all but the perfect trooper. The program knew how to push buttons and get the weak-willed to quit. Many who tried out for the program went in as egomaniacs and washed out as humbled servants to the cause.

There is silence in the room as she owns her post and Colonel Petzer stands facing the double doors, avoiding the plush leather chair to his left. After a few moments, the gatekeeper opens both doors, "He will see you now, sir." he says as he steps to the side, allowing space for the Colonel to enter. He enters at a military pace and hears both doors pulled closed behind him. The tension through them still to be felt.

"Welcome, Colonel Petzer, welcome. It is good to see you. I see you are prim and proper, as always. Perhaps soon we can talk you out of that uniform and into some civilian clothes?" Laughter from the Colonel is his only response.

Tension broken, Colonel Petzer speaks, "How are you, Chancellor?"

"Fine, fine." The Chancellor responds, waving at a set of plush leather chairs.

Colonel Petzer takes the offered seat, while the man across the desk speaks without hesitation, "I know you are a man of action, so I will get right to it. (He looks up at Colonel Petzer) I like that about you, by the way, not being one fuss with political words or waste time waxing poetic. I just assume when I enter a meeting, it will be two hours of beating around the bush and pretending there are no personal agendas by those in the room. The pleasantries of dealing with a military-minded man are refreshing to this person, in this position."

"I thought you were going to get right to it?" Colonel Petzer says, smiling.

"I rest my case." The Chancellor says.

"The good news is we received the unlimited funding we, I, was hoping for. I remember that request came from my mind now as I think about it, not yours: happy, happy, joy, joy on that fine piece of news.

The bad news is that the other three superior council members want to tour the facilities and possibly see a launch. Is that what you call it?"

"Sure, they can call it that if they want. Not sure that part is going to happen, though, John. I mean, anybody who isn't on that particular "launch" does not have clearance to be in the launch room or have authorization to know that one is or isn't taking place. Do you get my drift? If a tech crew member isn't assigned to that particular mission, they don't know of its existence. This includes other Tripper teams. Heck, the teams know that they exist but do not intermingle or live together; it is only the technicians that may actually interact with members of different tripper teams. This, in itself, is something I would like to rectify. Especially with your stellar news of unlimited funding, now we can become the modern-day version of the old American Navy Seal Teams. Unlimited funding and anonymity is why they rose to superiority amongst the world's special forces teams. I am ecstatic about the funding, great news!

However, three politicians visiting I am not a fan of. John, you know most politicians, no offense but, they will just be thinking how to take credit and take over. How to bend what we do to their personal advantage, not the greater good." Colonel Petzer says.

"I do take offense to that statement. This comes as no surprise to you; you know I am not one of those. Some of us sociopaths do rise to the top to expand our selfish mission of helping the greater good, create a sustainable system, and all that. Not all are run off greed and ego. Well, at least a different version of ego." He says, finishing in a laugh.

Colonel Petzer laughs and thinks hard. He knows his friend is right. Not all are bad, but yet, his alarm bells are going off, something negative will happen because of this visit. It may be a small price to pay in order to obtain unlimited funding, yet it may come at too high a cost. "Ok." he says at last. "You four can visit; give me a day or so to set it up." He knows it is Grey's team that will be leaving on that day. They are the soonest mission, and Colonel Petzer wants to get the politicians in and out as soon as possible. He doesn't want them to have time to come up with something stupid to do, not thinking about what Grey's mission is because it doesn't matter, yet still there is that nagging alarm bell in the back of his head.

"I know you well enough to know you are worried, Colonel. Just keep in mind, I am the one that is pushing for the funding. I want this program to succeed! I see the value of the project and the possible benefits to mankind. I also am not naive enough to think no-one will attempt to use this technology against us. Already others have a basic version of the technology, and as it develops and becomes refined and affordable, there will be a new version of history re-writing live."

Colonel Petzer thinks about that last statement for a minute. Perhaps a solid minute of thought, silence in the room as the Chancellor lets him think.

The Chancellor pours himself a drink, not one to drink this early, yet celebrations are in order. This program will silently keep him at the top; only a handful of people outside of the tripper program know of its existence. The fixes and tweaks the program will apply to history will continue to create a sense of happiness in his current time. That contentment will keep him in power. He sips his drink, thinking about how easy it is to rule people with psychology and the clear conscience to use the workings of the human mind to your advantage.

Colonel Petzer sits in his chair, thinking about the power he just gained and the responsibilities that go with it. If the tripper program is used for the wrong reasons, it can wreck the current ways of life. Who knows what the now or future will bring if the wrong people can screw with the past. He feels an absolute power run through his body, a surge through his chest —strength in the knowledge that he holds the power of the future in his hands. Heck, if he were power-hungry, he could seal off the underground facility after loading it up with years of supplies and reek hell with the history of all mankind. Colonel Petzer knows this is why the Chancellor picked him. Unlike many in positions of rank and power, the Colonel isn't driven by the need for position and power. Driven by honor and integrity, he is a different kind of dangerous.

"Are you in a hurry to get back?" the Chancellor asks, breaking the Colonel's chain of thoughts.

"Not particularly, the trip back doesn't take long and it's early yet. I ate on the way in, so I will probably seek out a couple people for catch up time before heading out.

"How about you, time for a cigar if you still have some?" Colonel Petzer asks.

"I do have some, but not the time." The Chancellor spins around in his chair and opens a drawer behind him. Extracting a humidor box, he turns back and presents the contents to Colonel Petzer. Peeking inside, the Colonel sees a random assortment of handcrafted cigars.

"Take a couple." The Chancellor says to him. Cigars are extremely hard to get these days, yet it is a celebration. Perhaps after the new current of funding is flowing strong, they can send a few tripper teams on some side missions solely to acquire some cigars. Of course, that is when all will realize things have changed.

Not shy about his love for strong cigars, Colonel Petzer first pulls a 60 gauge double maduro from the humidor. Sniffing it, he is satisfied with the smells of oak, oil, and dark roast coffee. Rolling it back and forth between two fingers, he feels the oils and a slight give to the surface of the cigar's wrapper. He looks in again and tilts his head at a particular cigar. He pulls out a torpedo-shaped one that alternates between a Connecticut and a maduro wrapper. Light and dark alternate up and down the thick cigar.

The Chancellor, after checking the humidistat, closes the humidor and returns it to its home. Spinning his chair back around, he sees the Colonel sniffing cigar number two. "Seems symbolic somehow, doesn't it. The blend of light-dark, good-bad, yin and yang."

"Indeed, it does." Colonel Petzer replies.

"Both have always existed, no reason to waste time wondering why. Just kick-the-ass of the other side every once in a while to keep everything in check and life is good." The Chancellor adds.

Colonel Petzer pulls open his Uniform jacket and stashes the two cigars inside. Everything else he needs to enjoy them is already contained therein.

Both men stand up and walk towards the double doors, turning towards each other, they grasp hands and shake the way people of mutual respect do. The Chancellor even puts his other hand on Colonel Petzer's shoulder; if he weren't a military man, the Chancellor might have escalated to a hug. Such is the elation he is feeling.

Sensing this thought, Colonel Petzer makes a hasty exit through one of the doors. Military men tend to tense up at the feeling of a hug, not cause they are afraid to touch, but because they have to remind their bodies that it is a sign of affection, not an attack. Throwing elbows at someone attempting to apply a hug does not go over well.

The Chancellor closes the doors behind Colonel Petzer. Whenever he meets with the Colonel, he is reminded of why he chose the Colonel for the program. A man full of integrity and a life-time of secret service to mankind is used to (word for invisible, not receiving recognition) and needs no accolades from the masses to thrive... .quite the opposite, really.

Now the Chancellor must deal with the other type of person, the other three superior council members. He knows they are driven by the desire to rule the world in their versions of utopia. Unfortunately, at least two of them are confirmed to be of the darker side of things.

Occasionally Colonel Petzer allows himself to utilize some perks of his position. This is one of those times.

Since he is at large and in charge, part of the deal is having a security detail with him when he is outside of secure areas. Between himself and the team of three who travel with him, any situation can be dealt with. The three troopers are a product of Colonel Petzer's training program. They are well versed in all types of warfare applicable to small teams. Now, in his current assignment, they are in no need of rank and he calls them all by their first names. Gail is a hard charger, and one who is always on point, not by assignment, her nature is thus. George is an anomaly; even his name doesn't seem to fit. All Colonel Petzer knows is he will do anything to accomplish his mission, anything. The third of his hand-picked team is Gordon; Gordon was not his birth name. Still, one he gained organically, both from his resemblance to a scientist turned badass from an ancient video game, and to his live version of the character, he can truly work a lab like the best of them, mostly to create cool explosives. Gordon can also pilot a boat, drive a buggy, or anything else with an engine. He is a crack shot and seems to be able to handle any weapon he picks up, as well as is strangely handy with a crowbar. Don't ask how we know about that last one....

Right now, the troopers and the two helicopter pilots are enjoying the perks of his position as well. They are lounging about near the helicopter. The female pilot and Gordon sit on the chopper's floor, feet dangling, chatting while the co-pilot and George are standing and talking. Gail, well she is watching over Colonel Petzer from afar, and not by his request.

Colonel Petzer sits on a limestone outcropping. He walked down to it from the sand and basalt rock blend that exists on the edge of this grandiose plateau. Halfway through one of the cigars, Colonel Petzer is doing what everyone in a position of power must do. He is thinking.

He thinks about the mission theme of the small units he ran in the past. He thinks about the mission of the trippers. Unsure he is at this point, uncertain of what the true mission of the trippers is. He became a great leader when he was able to accept that the mission of his troopers was not what they had engraved on the placard over the door, but to enforce and ensure the wants of those in power are met to their satisfaction, regardless of the end means of those wants.

Colonel Petzer sits here thinking on the Chancellor's wants, his real wants, not the words that leave his mouth. The Colonel knows when he figures that out, then he will see the tripper's true mission.

He looks across the vast valley strewn below him. The heated summer air is forced up and over the edge of this gigantic plateau, buffeted by the sheer rock, it races its heat towards the ponderosa pines behind him. Waving back and forth, they disperse the heat, creating a cooler environment just a few miles from the edge. Here where Colonel Petzer sits, enjoying the beginnings of a sunset, the winds are hot, drying his light and dark cigar quicker than he can smoke it. Inspecting it, he contemplates the balance that the Chancellor spoke about, his words were strange, yet the intention was clear, balance is the goal. Domination is for the bad guys.

The light softens and the hues embark on their evening mourning. The colors transition from sun-washed stark to pastels. Purples and azures replace dark blue in the sky, the heated air rising, cools as if a switch were turned, the expanses of the distant mountains hide the lower layers of light as he feels somebody coming. He knows it is Gail without looking.

"Its time Colonel." She says.

He looks at the cigar and takes a couple deep puffs before standing.

When he does, he walks over to where she is waiting close to the upward slope that will take them back onto the sands and basalts of the plateau, then a short way through the ponderosa pines to a clearing about 50 meters into the pines. There the helicopter blades are starting to move the air. No sounds are emitted from the technology powering the blades, only the wind they are creating, and the sudden silence of the forest creatures would indicate to anything that something is going on in this tiny section of the 200,000 square mile plateau. The perspective of that is magnitudinal.

All climb aboard the helicopter. The doors come closed as the pilot pulls on the stick, lifting the chopper from the ground, only the sounds of the debris scraping the surface of the earth and the clanking of tree branches against each other would alert those who want to know of their presence. A few grazing elk raise their heads in the distance, the emerging evening creatures pause in their tracks. Way off in the distance, a guard positioned high in an old tower swears they see a commotion in the forest. Looking towards the noise, nothing is seen but a bird disappearing into the distance.

Five

As the train comes to a screeching halt, John is already glad he made the efforts to make this happen. Who knows how long it would be before Grey approached him and said it is ok to go up top and party on. Probably never or maybe approaching Grey with the question is what told Grey he was ready, reaffirming that asking anybody, anything, at any time, is a good thing.

As the train zipped across the high desert valley, John watched out the windows as best he could. He grew up in a bubble city, probably very similar to the one he is about to spend the night in, although this time, John will be sleeping in the bottom tier of society. However, he was part of the revolution of his time as an undercover agent of sorts. They were living topside while secretly meeting and scheming in the service shafts of the between world, the area where the workers and servants living below performed their work. Not entirely up top, somewhere in between. Occasionally they were allowed to pop their heads up to upper levels to fix something, but only under extreme circumstances and with armed supervision.

Whenever John saw these worker bees, he would find a way to initiate a conversation with one of them. Always curious about their lives and what makes them tick. Usually, the security kept a close watch on him when he did so. Some of the recordings of these conversations were used to reinforce the testimony in his court proceedings, and it was a highly respected bottom dweller that turned him in. Loyal to the ones above, he overheard a couple of John's meetings with the rebels in the chambers of the in-between. But that is a story for another day. Today he is going to play.

John tries to remove the four-point harness, the images of the desert outside still being processed by his brain; after a brief struggle with the apparatus, he succeeds, gets up, and disembarks from the speed rail.

Charles and Rosa stand there waiting for him, "This is how you are already, and we haven't even gotten any alcohol into you yet!" she jokes.

Smiling, Charles stands like papa bear, grinning mischievously, as if you can't tell if he is proud of the cub stepping out or if he is getting ready to kill him to seduce momma bear back into estrus.

"This might be interesting," Charles says to Rosa, eliciting an elbow in the ribs.

"Behave." She says. "He's in shock."

John laughs, "A little bit. That train ride is something else. I never traveled like that before. In my time..."

"Quiet!" they both hiss at him.

John stops for a second, the reminder prevalent. He must be focused and conscious on this trip. Maybe treat it as work. His mouth has gotten him in trouble before.

"I got it." John says, "I got it. I just reset my brain to work mode. No more scoldings will be necessary, and that one was. I deserved that. Won't be necessary again." John, hyper serious, doesn't want to mess this up. The ability to come to town, the job, any of it. This life is way too fun.

Charles pulls John under his wing, squeezing John hard enough to elicit a wince. "I gotcha rookie, I gotcha."

John says, "Alright, alright," he smiles and walks with Charles and Rosa. This will be fun, a new culture, and getting to hang with these two in a different context will be a bonus, looking at them as something other than baby sitters.

Dirt and trash ... these are the first things that stand out to John as they take him wandering for a bit before going to their favorite bar. Even under this giant bubble, there is somehow a prevalence of dirt. How it finds its' way here is beyond him. Perhaps it filters its way down from above, things that are whole up there send their degrading fragments down to the street surface for him and the others to walk in.

No cars, buses, or public transportation of any kind exists within the lower levels of the city. His question about whether or not they have them above received shrugs from Charles and Rosa. Although allowed to do so, neither of them has ever felt the desire to party up top.

"Why not?" John asks.

"Not my people." is Charles' immediate response. "To many snooty people make me want to go postal on them all, their better-than-attitude drives me crazy. Noses in the air, too arrogant to see the shit their own feet are walking in. There is a reason most of my hits were on the upper class."

A man walking by gives him a sideways glance as he scurries down the street. Charles smiles, "Got one in mind, sir?" he asks him. The man breaks out into a gigantic smile, says nothing, nods, and keeps walking.

Rosa says, "John, it is different down here than you are thinking. This is not a world of mistrust and backstabbing and chaos and competition for resources. This is a self-contained and balanced, um, uh... what do you call it Charles?"

"Ecosystem, a balanced, sustainable ecosystem." Charles answers.

John looks at Charles.

"Don't say anything. He's into that shit." Rosa jokes.

"I think that is cool." John says, looking at Charles, "For reals. I look forward to talking to you about that stuff. I ... I am familiar with a human system that was billed that way, but really wasn't. The details of that are for home, though.

But beer, is that what you call it? And conversations sound great!" He says.

The streets are bustling and changing as they walk from the de-embarking area into a lesser area of the below. Even in balanced ecosystems, there are tiers of living. John finds it interesting, all of it. He considers himself a man of knowledge. Someday it will all click, and maybe he will present it in textbook form. No, in story form would be better!

Right now, though, he is being escorted towards a small, wooden facade building with these weird lights and signs adorning all the windows. Some flash slowly, while others just boldly proclaim, beer of champions, beer of Nascar, whatever that is... one has a blue bull on it, too many to describe.

They enter and make their way to a back corner booth.

Rosa makes John slide to the inside and sits on the end, while Charles claims the other side. Most of the room is located behind Charles' left shoulder.

John says, "First off, thanks for bringing me, this is stupendous already. And second, how is it Charles, you can sit with your back to this kind of room. I would think you would be one to want to see what is going on."

Charles grins and points at Rosa, "I trust her with my back first off. Second, when you come out of your corner, you will see mirrors on the wall. I can watch everything through those mirrors with more subtly than if I was looking directly about the room. It almost provides a filter; only the extreme stuff gains my attention. And three, no one is going to mess with us in here. The owner is a possessor of an iron hand."

Rosa leans in to whisper in John's ear. "He's a former tripper as well. He will know what you are just because you are with us."

"Wow, I can't wait to talk about it with him. I..."

Rosa's look interrupts him.

"Nothing will be said, ever." She says, "This is part of today's training, we don't exist, remember? We travel in and out by train from this facility. No one asks what we do out there. They are smarter than that."

"So much for the Utopian society!" John says.

"Actually, John, that is part of it." Charles says.

"Remember your history of the 1980s? Speaking of the '80s." Charles motions to his surroundings.

"Don't ask, don't tell was prevalent in the Militaries of certain countries, kind of a, keep me out of it, and all is good kind of a thing. Well, there is a lot of that here. And people don't complain about it because they are complacent in their happiness. Why should they worry and wonder about the goings-on when they are content?" Charles says.

John says, "One could say that is the goal and purpose of contentment."

Rosa laughs, "Yes. You two are going to have a great conversation while I get sloshed and kick some people's ass in darts."

The bartender comes up, delivering their favorite OV Splits. Looking at John, he simply nods. John nods back, enough said.

"Perhaps I can be your first victim? It's been a while since I've been beat." The bartender says. Friends with Charles and Rosa, he and Rosa have played many times.

Rosa gets up, wanting to leave John and Charles to their philosophy. She prefers action to talk.

* * *

John stands outside the bar, weaving ever so gently in a stationary circle. It has been a tremendous amount of time since he has consumed alcohol, and is not ashamed to say he is feeling the twelve "splits" consumed inside the bar. In fact, that is why he is standing out here, getting some fresh air. He looks up at the sky above and is reminded of the other culture existing above the heads of those living at the level he is vacationing at. It is a foreign land to him, not just because it's 2114 and everything has changed culturally, but because they seem more at peace down here than they did in his time. Or what he thinks of as his time.

He left in 2054, and his area of the world was in chaos. By the time he was acquired by the recruiters, even the upper echelons of his society were feeling the effects of the revolution. He is sure they were not happy about it either. The confirmation of this in his mind is why he had to disappear; it was fortunate timing that he was recruited to be a tripper. His former peers wanted to make an example of him and help temper the revolution by assassinating him and a few other key members of the revolution. Once the revolutionaries rescued him and some of the others, pulling a daring rescue during a between facilities transport. After that, his former peers skipped all formalities and killed the remaining revolutionaries in captivity. The story they pushed through the media was that they died while attempting to escape. John and his compadres know that their version of escape would have been putting their hands up as protection while they were being shot.

As John stands here weaving his stationary circle, content in his life, he wonders how many of them lived another day, the key members of the revolution that is. He is sure no others are alive today. It was a tough choice for him to leave them behind, yet knowing the truth, he, like all the others, was dead if he stayed. He was a possible future martyr and too dangerous not to kill now and use him as an example to all who live in the upper tiers to not help the revolutionaries.

John is not sure if it is his neck craned in a weird position, the beers, or the thoughts that cause the nausea; he doesn't have time to decide before it overwhelms him. Bringing his head to level, he looks frantically left and right, before seeing a small space between the wall of the bar and the building next door. John hurries into the gap, seeking a private place to empty his stomach. He finds himself alone with a multitude of containers and piles of empty cases of beer. He projectile vomits onto the side of the building. Three times.

His stomach now empty, John stands for a moment recovering, his face hot, tears in his eyes. He wants to wait for his body to go back to normal and his vision to clear before going back inside to tell Charles and Rosa he is done for the night, time for him to go to the accommodations to recover. First, they need to tell him where it is!

He hears a voice through the pounding in his head, "Rough night?" it says.

Through bleary eyes, John looks towards the voice. Peering back at him through intense eyes is a man bent over, hands on his knees, staring back intently. Not with concern, but hunger.

"Go away, I am fine." John squeaks at the man.

The man jerks his body backward at John's response. He straightens his body at tall as it will go. A curvature of his back preventing a proper human posture.

He says, "I am merely checking on you, my man."

"I don't believe you." John squeaks back. Another round of vomit is attempting to escape, the bottom dregs of the sour liquid mixture of bile and beer is ready to be released.

John takes a purposeful step backward and releases it onto the ground between him and the strange man.

The stranger has no reaction. He waits.

John groans, hunched over, a hand on each lower thigh for support; he uses the support to push himself upright. The last liquid removed, he will feel better soon. Right now, he is struggling.

The man is still there, hunched over from practice, he watches John, a hat held in his hands. It seems he wants to see inside John's soul. Uncomfortable by the effort, Johns waves him away.

The man is still as a statue.

As John's eyes come into focus, he can see the details of the intrusive man. He is wearing the same style of clothes as the rest of the locals. Beige in color, made of well-crafted cloth, although they seem brand new, covered in dirt they are. The man also is covered in the dirt, his balding head contains a ring of hair circling around the back of his head from one ear to the other, brown and greasy, it appears curly and frees itself in all directions, perfection in its chaos. He clutches a hat in his hands; John doesn't remember seeing anyone with a hat. Strange.

John breaks the silence.

"Look, sir, it seems you are looking for something I cannot provide. I do not swing that way, and although I can understand the draw, even in my current condition, I simply have to say no and good day. "

The man laughs, a forced, loud ruckus. "Haahaa HA!" bemusement overwhelms his face for a moment.

"Duly noted, my inebriated friend. What is it that brings you to the enclosed tomb that is Namazinga-2? I can see you are not from here, are you from that (he uses air quotes audaciously) secret base located on the other side of the valley? Occasionally when the air is super clear, like in the winter, we swear we see helicopters flying back and forth from the train depot located out there."

John, even in his current state, is smart enough to ignore the question. His alarm bells are going off in all directions. Peering through bleary eyes, he knows this person who appears as a homeless alley dweller, is not.

"What is a helicopter?" John slurs.

The man guffaws in laughter and steps closer, encompassing John's vision; John attempts to step back and stumbles on his own heel. He sees an arm reach out and feels the stranger's hand grip his shirt with surprising strength. Enough to prevent John from falling.

"Careful young man, in your state, you may get hurt if you aren't more careful. Now how about not lying to me...lets put that high IQ of yours to good use." Venom through his lips.

How does he know about John's IQ? If John was sober, he might have let his ego get the best of him, but luckily he was tanked and saw through the ego stroke.

John decides to use the fight training Rosa is putting the rookies through, not of the natural physical type. It is a stretch for him. He throws a lazy elbow at the stranger. The stranger pushes John away with the hand already gripping his shirt at his chest, the elbow swings haphazardly between the two men. John's weight is now wholly on the back of his heels; the only thing preventing him from falling over backward is the hand gripping his shirt. He is thinking about swinging at the arm so it will release, and he can fall backward when the hand pulls him back towards the stranger. An explosion rocks his head, again and again. It takes a moment for him to realize he is being punched. The arm then pushes him back again, so all his weight is on his heels.

John knows what is coming. He has been tortured for information before and can feel that type of energy coming from this non-alley-bum. John feels helpless and prepares himself for a beating, knowing he will never tell this man what he wants to know. John may be a goofball, but he is a badass goofball.

The man repeatedly asks John questions that he already knows the answer to, he has to, otherwise John's IQ may step through the drunken stupor and put two and two together. First, he must get John to answer these types of questions before asking the ones he really wants the answers to. After about five minutes of questions, punches, and kicks applied to John, he decides to take him to a more secure location. It will not be long before someone hears the commotion, or this dude's buddies come looking for him.

Retaining his grip on John's shirt, he stands and drags John towards the alley's bowels. He feels more than sees a small figure appear at the street end of the alleyway. Looking over his shoulder, he sees a short, tight, substantial presence of a human standing there. He drops John with no hesitation and takes off at a practiced, stooped over, damaged goods type of run. At least until he rounds a corner into another alley that is, then he stops his act and runs full bore. Escape is his intent.

Charles sitting at the booth, waiting for John, is concerned. John has been gone too long and is probably passed out outside. Just as likely, he is outside trying to pick up one of the local women, or all of them.

Charles gets up from his seat and walks to where Rosa, playing darts, is kicking everybody's asses per usual. "Hey, I'm going to go check on John. He went outside for fresh air and never came back." He says to her.

"I'm coming with you." She replies without hesitation. As soon as Charles approached her, her trained instincts knew something was wrong. They both leave the bar and outside, look left and right. To the right is a long line of buildings, across the street is an alley and to their left is one as well. Not seeing John anywhere, they go left to check that one.

Rosa, moving her little legs at a military pace, gets to the end of the alley first. As soon as her eyes adjust to the dark, she sees John being beaten by a bum who is holding him by his shirt. There is no resistance from John. She takes off into the alley.

Charles reaches the alley a split second after Rosa runs into it. Rounding the corner, he sees Rosa run by John in pursuit of a man. Although Charles can't quite place who or why but, the fleeing figure seems familiar. Perhaps he was a customer at the bar, and he saw him there, although he seemed more familiar than that. Maybe it's the hat, the man in all his efforts to escape, still wanted to put his hat back on his head. Filing the note in his brain for later, he turns his focus on the team member lying on the ground. Since Rosa was already in hot pursuit, it is his job to get John back on his feet.

"How you doing, buddy?" Charles asks.

"I'm good, well, other than feeling like I got hit by an Autobot."

"A what?" Charles asks.

"Autobot." John slurs.

"Well, ok, buddy, you'll have to explain that to me later. First, let me do a body check. I want to make sure nothing is broken. Are you ok?" he asks John again.

"When in doubt, please refer to the previous statement." John says. After a standard field body check, Charles knows John will fine. Not great, but ok.

Rosa chases the figure down the alley. It is amazing to her that no matter what time-frame they are in, alleyways exist! It seems humans always want a way to keep their dirtier side hidden from strangers. They all have it, a dirtier side, a shadow, a dark side, yet chose to hide it from each other, in most cultures at least. Some do choose to celebrate it.

Rosa refocuses her brain's attention. She has to save the philosophy and book mind for her time off. Right now, she is chasing some asshole down the back alleys of Namazinga-2. He is fast too.

She turns up her afterburners a little and starts to gain ground on him. When he rounds a corner, she rounds the same corner a second later. The man no longer is stooped over and is sprinting now! As he runs, his hat flies off, revealing long red hair, free from the cover. The hair flows with his speed, stretching out behind him. It is the last thing she sees as he rounds a corner ahead of her.

Rosa hurries to catch up to the man. She knows he is a man despite the long red hair, unusual in 2114, the long hair that is. Rosa still knows he is a man by the way he runs. His clothing seems time-frame appropriate best she can tell from a distance, plain and non-distinct. Rosa rounds another corner, once around, she gets a good view of what she is turning into. A long street presents itself in front of her, an utterly empty main-drag.

Slowing her pace, she jogs a long way down it before deciding to turn back.

Taking a break from the running, she walks back. Looking nonchalant, her senses are on high alert. Her peripheral vision is seeking out movement. Her ears are listening for heavy breathing or the scrape of clothing on a wall, something to indicate a person in hiding. And her sixth sense is prepared and ready to raise the hairs on the back of her neck if the necessity arises.

As she turns back into the alley where it all started, she is thinking how weird it is that John was attacked; she and Charles have never had an issue here before. In fact, most of the city dwellers just pretended they didn't exist. Strangers in a big city are experts at ignoring each other.

"How is he?" she asks when she gets to John and Charles.

"He will be fine. I think we should abandon the visit to take him back and get him to medical, though. We have a mission in a couple days and need him in mission shape. Grey will want to know what happened, as well." Charles says.

Rosa nods, then they both help John to his feet. As they walk him back to the bar, Rosa tells Charles about the person she pursued, how he lost his hunchback and her with ease. She also described his hair and physical details, the ones she noticed while running after him. The policewoman in her notices things by training, even while chasing them down alleys. Especially while chasing them down alleys.

After settling up at the bar, the three head to the train station, none of them notice a figure far down the street peeking at them from the end of an alley. The human figure watching them smiles. He may have failed to gain any information from John, would have been surprised if he had actually, but he did have a lot of fun. He will enjoy the next couple of weeks tremendously!

Six

Miokel thrives in the private space of his quarters. With everything he did to it, one wouldn't know he lives hundreds of feet underground. He painted windows on the wall, the windows, surrounded by curtains long and deep red, help accentuate the scene drawn beneath.

The two window paintings match and are grandiose in image. Created in such a way that it seems the room is perched on a rock stone cliff, standing watch over a deep valley below. Trees tall enough to sway just beneath the level of the window sill, stretch long and straight racing for the sky, their bark is feathery and leathery as it strains to keep up with the growth, remnants shag in all directions. They can be imagined flapping in the breeze as the bark waves for a bird's attention to be grabbed and further utilized as a weatherproofing for their nest and young-ins.

The valley pulls away to the left in one painting and to

56

the opposite in the other. The room stands on the pinnacle of the hill, looking east and west, respectively. One can easily imagine the sun rising in one window and setting in the other. Miokel does this frequently, and often, it is his morning and evening ritual when he is not on a tram-ride.

Miokel's reputation and Grey's help them get him an apartment in the complex's quietest area. Miokel's residence is tucked into an alcove one floor below Grey's and off to the side of the commons. The design of the place happened to create a dead spot as far as sound goes. When he stands on the balcony that his and every quarters has, he looks across one side of the commons and slightly back towards a bulk of the other apartments. Since his place starts after a large curve and apartment-less area of the structure, there is a large gap between his and the next balcony. The in-between was created millions of years before the humans built this structure; the natural limestone lay untouched by human hands, creating a natural barrier between Miokel and the next apartment. Over the years, either through nature's persistence or just as likely, human intervention, birds and squirrels made their way down into the underground complex. Too far below the surface to walk, they would have had to hitch a ride on a helicopter and elevator to get here. Miokel is glad they did. He stands on the right edge of the balcony nearest the cliff and throws scraps of food absentmindedly while thinking about his theories and ideas.

Miokel is on a mission. A mission to discover the variations in history to document the different perspectives of history. He doesn't like the one view perspective that most go with. He remembers his schooling and his fellow classmates. Whenever they would study something and read from a recorded work, he noticed his fellow students would believe whatever they read first. He did not. He does not accept the one view perspective of history. Just cause someone from, say England documents an event, interaction, political altercation, or battle with another country, it doesn't make the other country's document history invalid. One must study all perspectives from all sides and all documentation of it: newspaper, history books (even they vary greatly), personal memoirs. Outsider's opinions and perspectives are something he brings into his research as well.

One-quarter of his apartment is dedicated to said research. He has areas to hang perspectives and thoughts, using string to connect the dots between papers and pictures. Piles of information, contained in various forms, lay about on two big tables he has placed there. His brain is always working on many theories simultaneously. The apparent haphazard piles of papers, books, and tablets are actually his organization of different events and perspectives of those events.

This is what Miokel does in his spare time. This is what he is doing right now. They returned from their last mission four days ago, he's been at it for most of those days. Their experiences on the last mission offered a new perspective of his research around what history calls World War One or WW1. Since he returned, he has worked to fill in unknown areas of history. No Lee Batard exists in history, Mata Hari and Agros Petros both appear. The legionnaire chief he met and liked tremendously met his end in the battles to come; in fact, most of the Armenian French foreign legion died during the war. As did the Ottoman empire. Not much is documented on either. It is hard to see the long term effects of incidents, wars, government overthrows, Coups, deaths of great leaders, assassinations, etc. Miokel, however, considers these long term connections. The dots draw lines in his brain between the separate events, and as he lives his life, they come up with theories and seek out holes in the theories as Miokel goes about his day and missions. It is a separate and active subconscious that quietly does its thing until it lets off a DING when it finds something important.

While getting cleaned up from said last mission, Miokel's brain gave him a DING! Perhaps it was assisted by the AED's electricity, forced into resolution, knowing that someday Miokel will die, so if it wants the truth to be told, the time is now.

The smuggling of goods through the area they just returned from had to come from somewhere. The flow of crates, food, and other products was constant the entire time he and the rest of the team were in that tiny, unknown, Mediterranean shore town. A lot of value in all that product and a significant loss to some countries fighting their wars.

Miokel is standing there between the two tables, lost in thought when his apartment door opens. The change in air pressure gains his attention immediately, and he looks with no-worries. He is expecting Grey to stop by. Long ago, Grey was given access to his apartment.

"Hey." Miokel says, looking up from his work.

"Miokel, how are you?" Grey walks into Miokel's work zone, and they shake hands affectionately.

"I'm great." Is Miokel's absentminded response.

Grey nods his head and looks around at Miokel's passion. He looks forward to reading Miokel's memoirs and findings someday. He knows his brain is powerful and passionate about connecting the dots.

"What have you been up to these last four days? Where did you go this time?" Miokel asks.

He is referring to the virtual reality system all the apartments come with. Miokel's sits dusty, while Grey's is polished with use. Miokel's research and thoughts are his escape, while the virtual reality system is Grey's favorite thing to do while recovering from the time travel's "jet lag."

"I was in need of a little R & R, so I laid in a hammock strung from a sideways growing palm tree. The hammock is only dry accessible at lower tides, so if you climb in before the tide comes in, you have no choice but to stay in the hammock until the tide goes back out. Well, unless I wanted to swim, but why would I want to do that when I can sleep and sway just above the surface made of turquoise glass and dangle a finger in it to cause ripples that disappear into the distance." Grey says.

"Nice! Anything in the water?" Miokel asks.

"Just a couple of dolphins, not much else, they would occasionally swim up and say hello. One even rested its chin on my belly a couple of times, once they got used to me, that is."

They both are aware that it is really Grey's brain that had to get used to the idea. His belief systems and past experiences determine the boundaries since the system runs off his thoughts and instincts, as well as what he consciously tells it to do. One knows the system is working right when the user forgets this fact.

"What have you been working on Miokel?" Grey looks at the piles of stuff and wonders how he keeps track of it all. He is guessing it is some combination of his brains and the way he places and stacks everything.

"Uh, not much. Just connecting some dots around wartime commerce and who it helps and who it doesn't.

Seeing all those goods moving through that shore town has me wondering where it all was coming from. Which countries were being pilfered while they were busy fighting to retain their borders?

Based on the types of things I saw or smelled, the produce, hay, guns, you name it, gives me clues as to their origin. I simply research where it is possible to grow or make certain things, and use deductive reasoning to combine past research in my brain or do more as necessary, to give me a good idea where the item came from." Miokel says.

"Well, where do you think it was coming from, any conclusions yet?" Grey asks.

"All of them."

"All of them?" Grey asks.

"Yes, all of them. Whoever was running that smuggling operation had the ability to gain materials from either side of the war. Money driven, not loyal to any particular country, all about free enterprise. Loyal to their business, not a country of origin." Miokel says.

"Maybe their own country. Maybe they were from a country that wasn't involved in the war while we were there. Or a country that was a forced ally of sorts. Like a colony." Grey says.

"Exactly. That is a strong idea!" Miokel smiles at Grey, and then stares at a pile of papers. He is heading back into that place of thought. Grey seeing this, wants to give him his last day of rest.

"We have today, and then tomorrow we are back at it again. I meet with Colonel Petzer first thing in the morning. Will you meet with the rest of the team at nine and run them through some IED and AED drills?" Grey smiles at his use of acronyms back to back. Miokel doesn't react to his smile as he is staring at his work, although he may have heard it in Grey's voice. "Yes, I will remind them how to kill someone and how to revive someone. Or did you mean how to disarm an explosive device?" Miokel asks.

"Dismantle. We will go over creating them some other time. Besides, I don't know if I am ready to teach John how to blow things up!" There's that smile again.

Miokel looks up from his work this time. Happy to hear

the joy in his long-time friend's voice. He wants to see it. Glad to see it.

"Me either. Mackenzie maybe? She has it in her." Miokel says.

"True, but we can talk about that later. Let's enjoy the rest of our day off." Grey says.

"Sounds good. I'll see you after your meeting then. Here's to another good mission; I wonder when we are going this time?" Miokel says.

"I have no idea." Grey says as he walks towards the apartment door, once again admiring Miokel's apartment on the way. The wall adorned with those two giant painted windows, collected items, and hangings decorating the rest of the walls. Nary a piece of concrete is to be seen. The sky mural on the roof is his most favorite. The bright azure, mixed with milky white clouds, shorten the apartment in its vastness.

Reaching the door, Grey opens it and lets in a few faint hums and other soft sounds of machinery. Other than that, Miokel's apartment's location eludes a clean back alley type of feeling when you exit it. The surreal transition from design to the stark mediocrely-lit hallway, emits a sense of dusk when stepping into it. Grey decides to turn right and take the maintenance stairs the one flight up to his quarters instead of the elevators to the left. He will figure out what to do with his day when he gets back to his place.

Seven

The four politicians stand at the observation window; they are the first four humans not involved in the project ever, getting to see the program's intimate workings. Looking below, they see seven tiny figures walk up a short flight of stairs and assume a bowling pin sort of formation. The distance and vibrating window make it hard to notice the details of the humans below. The grizzly bear rumble of the giant machine that consumes one entire wall of the room below works it's way into the control room. A voice speaks behind them; it is Loren. He once again is in charge of the technical aspects of a mission, only his second time.

"Even though this room is isolated from the machine, we still feel the vibrations created during wind up and wind down. Once it is up to running speed, the vibration seems to even out, and the giant springs this room sits upon are enough to isolate the vibrations." Loren says.

The politicians look at each other, not entirely understanding what the technician means. Seeing this, he continues. Colonel Petzer said his job was to distract the visitors and make sure they don't notice too many intimate details of their operation, the less they notice, the better. So it is his intention to keep them lost in more information and geek speak, without them learning anything essential or pertinent to their overall mission. Easy peasy.

"This room was built similar to the control rooms of the missile silos America and Russia had during their Cold War. It was not called a cold war because of the temperatures where they lived, but because like an angry couple, they pretended they weren't mad at each other and instead performed covert undermining missions on each other." Loren waited for their laughter, yet none came. "The room sits on gigantic springs and is literally suspended in the air, the floor, ceiling, and three walls are independent from the rest of the structure. The window and wall you are standing next to is one section of the rest of the structure. If you look at the wall's seams, you will see hard rubber edges where the suspended room interacts with the rest of the structure. This is why when you look through the window, you experience some of the vibration coming from the machine, about 2% of the vibration to be exact."

He receives a few nods from the politicians.

From behind him, "Sir?" Loren will have to get used to being called sir, now that he is in charge.

"Yes?" he responds. Then he realizes what the next question is, "Yes, they are ready below." Loren addressing the visitors, "You'll have to excuse me for a minute, I have to communicate with the tripper team standing below."

He assumes the staring off into space look that everybody gets when talking into a communications device.

"We are a go up here. Are you a go?" Loren asks.

The viewers see the figure in the front turn to look at the six people standing behind him. He turns back as they hear the technician speak, "Roger that." Then the visitors hear him say what Loren's team of technicians will soon recognize as his signature phrase, "Let her rip."

The technician sitting in Loren's former seat pushes a few keys with his fingers and, with his own version of flare, pushes a final key that informs the giant machine to take action.

It takes a few seconds for any detectable action to be seen below. Before that, the visitors all notice a sharp rise in static electricity. Below, the electricity is pronounced; it emanates towards them through the viewing window. One of the visiting politicians, a tall woman with striking features and dark hair, leans a bit too close to the glass, intending to get a better look at the figures below. Her nose touches the reinforced glass, and the electricity reaches out to her. ZAAAP! She receives an electric shock from the glass, it startles her, and she revolts backward. A flash of anger crosses her face and then a smile. She steps back close to the glass again and touches her finger to it several times in a row, each time it gifts her with a ZAAAP! Now that she is expecting it, she thrives on the feeling. A piece of paper lifts its way upwards in front of the window, removing her from her play. She sees dust and scraps of paper twirl about the room on the other side of the glass, the electricity creating a tornado of energy. The far wall melts without warning and spins itself in a clockwise direction; it looks like something she made on a paint wheel at a fair once, drips of paint applied to a spinning piece of paper creating memories.

All four visitors are encapsulated with the energy finding its way through the window to them; they watch with a child's fascination, while their adult minds attempt to find reason and logic. Without warning, the seven figures blur and disappear into the vortex existing in the formerly solid wall. After a moment more, they hear their guide, the lead technician for this mission says, "They're good, shut her down."

The wall un-moltens and becomes solid before their

eyes, the papers and dust drop out of sight, and the room below becomes still as a few stubborn items find resting places. The room, full of excitement a moment ago, now is stale and boring. The visitors turn away with a look of surprise and excitement glued to their faces. Loren thrives on the reaction, and with a mental reminder of his mission with them today, promptly starts talking again as he leads them from the room, lest they learn any details of the mission, like where the team time-traveled off to.

"Follow me if you would, and we will give you a short tour of some other parts of the facility. You have seen the reason for the season. Now, let's see some of the things that support the reason and help make it happen." Loren says to them as he whisks them out of the room. All of them sneak a peek at the technicians sitting in front of computer screens, doing who knows what, but it is obvious they are focused on their tasks.

The visitors do not realize the tech's are avoiding interaction with the strangers who might ask them questions they are not allowed to answer, and would have to risk insulting them by informing them of their oaths of secrecy. It is better to not interact at all with those that are giving the program unlimited funds. Yes, of course, they have heard the rumors and scuttlebutt. And yes, of course, they want unlimited funding, each for their own selfish reasons.

Eight

The team finds themselves once again in the year 1917. Once again, the Kangal Dog is their next-door neighbor. The team takes the time to say hello. He, currently protecting a flock of sheep, was not friendly at first. Once he recognized their smell, his body language quickly switched from go away to the full-body wag that a dog assumes when it sees an old friend.

The team were not sure if they are here before or after their last visit, now they have confirmation that they are indeed here later in time than their previous tram-ride to the area. Not sure how much later, the team is super careful and aware as they leave the walled-in yard space's safety and step into the alleyway that creates a pathway from street to street. The alley is as dirty and stinky as last time they were here. The locals still throw their garbage and human waste into it, forcing Rosa to lift her skirt to avoid more contact with it. Of course, it is not until she sees Mackenzie and June lift their skirts to avoid the offal that she thinks to do the same, preventing any further fecal matter from coating the bottom edges of her dress.

The damn dress has her feeling free and vulnerable once again.

All seven work their way through the trash and approach the end of the alley; their goal is the cafe they visited last time. Grey thinks it will be a safe place to hang out for a bit. He hasn't yet told the team that they have two missions while here, with a day off in between. He wonders what kind of trouble John will get into with a day off in an exotic land. Grey just hopes he doesn't flirt with the wrong woman and get himself beheaded.

The team's first mission is simple, and then after a day off, they are to acquire some kind of scroll from one of the lesser bosses of the man they stole jewels and rocks from last time they were here. Grey knows the markings on the outside and the pattern on the deep red, wax seal. This second mission was a last-minute addition, even Miokel doesn't know the details of it yet.

The team works its way along the streets of the port town. Like any port town, it is full of a diverse mix of sailors and merchandise. The variety of humans here helps them walk without notice to the cafe. They arrive to see it is the same utilitarian environment as last time. The owner recognizes them and welcomes them back, "Ah, yes. Welcome, welcome." He greets them as if they spent vast amounts of currency the last time they were in, or perhaps he just likes them. He takes their order, and after a few minutes, returns with their beverages. Their food will take a bit longer. The team naturally pauses their conversation while he deposits drinks in front of everyone. After a bit too long of silence, everyone notices he is on pause and staring at June. Of course, this happens to her everywhere she goes, even in a port town like this one. The stark contrast between the beige stucco behind her and the bourbon red of her curly locks entices a glow to surround her head, not so much as a halo but as an overall body glow that just makes people, men and women, want to stare. When she talks and story-tells, they all pause life for as long as it takes for her to finish her story.

Right now, no one is telling a story. Instead, June, realizing he won't go away until she acknowledges him, looks up and says. "Hi." Inducing a body inducing melt of thought and reason, the cafe owner blushes through his dark skin and nods his thanks at her for her greeting. He then flees the scene.

"I guess we are going to have to get used to that." Miokel jokes.

"Me too, I'm not used to the competition. Usually, all eyes are on me. Even though I am not gay, it is strange that he is not making eyes at me." John says and looks at June, "I will have to step up my game!"

Grey shakes his head. John is an interesting character, to say the least, hard to describe or explain. He is narcissistic as hell and yet will literally let you stand on his back during a mission...for any reason. No questions asked, John will do whatever it takes to help out the team. Yet, he is a different creature when not on a mission, or in "mission mode," kind of like now. We are on task, yet he is light of mood. A great trait for long term excellence as a tripper. As comfortable on mission as off. Or in John's case, more at home on mission. Perhaps, it is the only time he allows all of him to show up, instead of the mask he wears the rest of the time?

The team is waiting for Grey to start. All are curious as to their mission here. As always, Grey keeps the details to himself and Miokel until they tram-ride to their mission time frame. Security is important.

Grey feels their impatience, "Ok, I was going to wait for the lamb stew and unleavened bread to arrive, but we can start. The silence is killing me." He smiles.

"We actually have two separate missions this time. The first one is a simple "observation mission" or "recon" as some would say. The second one is..."

He pauses as the food arrives, the timing impeccable. The cafe owner and a women they have not seen before bring all seven bowls of stew at once. This time the woman sneaks many peeks at June; it seems this is half the reason she is helping. They speak in their native tongue to each other as they work. A few sentences in, those graced with nano-chip auto translators raise their eyebrows at something they say. Other than that involuntary reaction, they give nothing away until they leave.

"Did I hear that, right?" Rosa asks.

Charles and Miokel nod in reply.

Mackenzie, June, and John, not eligible for their auto translators until after this, their third mission, are in the dark.

John speaks, "What did they say? They obviously said something, a few of you reacted to something they said. It would be gnarly if you would share it with us three."

Charles looks at John, "Not the context I would have used, but nicely done." while hanging in the bar prior to John's back alley experience Charles and John were exchanging words. Charles is looking forward to slipping in the phrase "why eat when you can drop it in" a reference to how the people in John's time frame get their nutrients. In 2054 there are no natural foods. All the necessary ingredients for human survival are manufactured and replicated through the use of chemistry and science.

The other word, John taught him, he will have to save for his lover and used to be therapist. She is still a therapist, just not his, although she does deliver his medicine for him. He has been on natural medicines to deal with his PTSD and insomnia; he uses less of it now that he has talked to someone about his past, someone that is nonjudgmental about it. The THC he induces through his lungs helps to relax the part of his brain that is always alert to the possibilities that someone is going to kill him or that a killer is in the room, or...the list goes on. Hyper-vigilance gets to rest a bit when he can utilize modern natural medicines. He uses it as anyone would use a prescribed medication, a dose at a time, and at regular intervals. It is why he carries it in his chest pocket. Always there as needed.

Grey answers John's questions finally, after a bit of thought, "They were talking about June. He said, "See, it is her." The woman responded, "It is not, she has dark skin and red curly hair, this woman is pale-skinned."

"What are they talking about?" June wants to know.

"I don't know either. I am curious, though." Grey responds.

"Well, I feel better. It is a case of mistaken identity. Perhaps he will still lust for me, perhaps she will as well." John says.

Charles, an image of the five by five, homely woman in his head, shudders at the picture attempting to enter his brain of her and John, add in the cafe owner and ugh.

Rosa steers them back towards the mission at hand, "You were going to tell us about the first mission?

Grey nods his head, filing the overheard tidbit of information in one of his "for later" files of his brain.

"This time, we will split up into a few teams and spend some time gathering data for the PABs (Powers that Be). According to Colonel Petzer, they are intrigued by the amount of items moving through this area. It is not something searchable by their computers, and apparently not noted by any human timeline. So we are to observe and report as they say. Spend a day gathering data on what types of goods move through here. Providing them with items will help them figure out where it is all coming from."

"How is that important enough to send us 200 years back in time to find out?" John asks.

Miokel wonders the same.

Grey simply shrugs his shoulders; he gave up trying to figure out how they thought many years ago. It makes it easier. All he knows is they are here to observe and report. He is glad for the simple first mission, considering the second one. Perhaps this tram-ride is really about the second mission, and it is not an add-on, as Colonel Petzer says. The Colonel is straight up, though. He would tell Grey what is up, even if his superiors didn't want him to. Grey knows this already.

"We are going to split the rookies up. John, you will be with Charles, Rosa and Mac will team up, and that leaves Miokel and June together. You two (pointing at June and Miokel) will be reconnecting with that Armenian Legionnaire that helped us last time we were here. Let's see if he is more comfortable with us this time and willing to provide us with some details that he knows and didn't want to say before. Rosa and Mac are to wander the town proper and see what type of information you can gather, while Charles and John head to the docks." Grey says.

"That leaves you with nothing to do, Mr. Grey. Will you be napping or getting lai..." a look from Grey shuts John sentence off, a bolt of lightning type of shut down.

"I will be going to the house where Rosa and I acquired the jewels and rocks from last time we were here. I bet that guy is the reason for the season, as they say. I'm going back into his office to see what type of paperwork he has, if any, and to peruse the grounds to see what I find.

We will commence right after our meal.

Remember, observe and report, not interact and steal, as much as possible, don't get too close to anyone, and don't be inappropriate." Grey finishes by looking at John, who puts his best innocent face on.

At this point, the exotic spices, lamb, and broth scents wafting around in the cool breezes entering through the glassless windows ends any further conversation as, on a silent signal, they all devour their stew and unleavened bread. From the kitchen, those with translators can hear the discussion continue at a louder volume than before, "It is her." "No, she is dark, not light."

Nine

The Sheik sits and sips his tea; it is quickly becoming his favorite time of day. Being the Sheik definitely has its privileges. He is sitting here drinking the finest tea in the world and listening to the strange system his marauders had acquired a few weeks ago. After much torture and persuading, the previous possessor was convinced to show the Sheik how it works. The strange heavy rectangular objects were identified as "batteries." They are necessary to "power" the device he called a "radio."

He turns the dial slowly. He is learning that if he goes slow, he is more likely to not miss some sounds going across the radio. His favorite so far is the one that the music came across. It is incredible to hear sounds out of thin air that usually take an extreme effort for him to listen to. Even as powerful as he is, it still takes a supreme effort to get an orchestra anywhere near him. Or a long strange trip to the land of the British, the areas of his country they are slowly turning into white abominations of its former self.

But then there is the music; he loves the strings. The string instruments are nothing but soul coming forth from the person holding it. He wonders if they die young from giving all their soul to the instrument. They are not the only ones to do so. Die young, that is, the souls that die young for him are the ones he respects the most.

Slowly turning the dial, he happens across some voices. Turning it back a little, he makes the sound a little clearer.

"...After the probation period, Mac. Which lasts for three missions, then is waiting for my report on you three. It is mostly done by the way. When we return, I will finish them that day and put in the requests for you three to have the surgery." Grey says.

"Great!" Mackenzie says.

""Oh, and I wouldn't say, standing there and looking pretty isn't doing... "

Wait! Does he know that voice, is it familiar to him? It is...but how could it be? It has been so long since he heard it that he doubts that its possessor is the strange exotic tall man he remembers from his youth. The one that stood there tall and stone-faced while his partner was drawn and quartered. He had either seen it before or didn't really like the man at all based on his lack of reaction to the whole event.

The Sheik pours some more tea and settles into his nest of pillows. Smelling the three women nesting together nearby, he is reminded of his nightly duties. Deciding instead to listen to the radio, he lets them snuggle together, keeping each other warm from the cool desert air. He needs to know if this is indeed the exotic stranger from his younger years. It has been 20 years since that incident, but that voice and period of his life will always be remembered. It was early in his campaign to run this region; he was out marauding and came across a group of seven strange people wandering lost, or so they initially said. He ended up killing four of them and letting the other three go after coming to terms with them on some things. As he sits here now older and wiser, he wonders if they had been sent here to come to those terms.

The Sheik listens to find out more.

"Rosa, how you two doing?" he asks.

"Well, you know. We've learned how to ask for sex in a multitude of languages..." Rosa says through the comms.

John interjects, "I will be needing that information later." he says.

"Other than that, we found out this stuff comes from everywhere, the ships converge here, are unloaded, then the goods are carried to various...

The pot of tea the Sheik consumed while listening to the music commands him to relieve himself. Walking out into the fresh night air, he looks up at the desert's megadose of stars and wonders what they are all about, besides giving him something to do while emptying his bladder. As the Sheik finishes, he wonders what to do next. He listened to the radio voice long enough to remove all doubt as to the owner of the voice. He knew it the second he first heard it somehow: now what to do about it? He would love to have a conversation with this man again, what was his name... Hmm, it will come back to him. In the meantime, "Hakeem!"

Hakeem arrives instantly, "Yes."

The Sheik walks up to the three women waiting there patiently for him; they would wait forever. "Send two scouts in all four directions. Not sure what they will find, tell them to look for things out of place and have one ride back to inform us and the other to stay, track and leave sign for us."

"Yes, sheik." He leaves to set the command in motion. Two riders in each direction, sent north, south, east, and west to find who knows what. Hakeem has no doubt they will find something; the Sheik is all-knowing after all. Or just un-ego'd enough to listen to his instincts.

The Sheik puts his arms out, two of the chosen three stand to help disrobe him, the third just moves a little closer, staying on her knees, in the ready for him.

He stands there thinking, making the woman's job tougher. They all want to father his first child. None have been that fortunate as of yet, try as they might. The firstborn will rise to power, and so will they along with him. Such is the importance that twice now, members of the harem were forced to abort their pregnancies. If they were strong enough to fight off the jealous women or sneaky enough to hide it longer, then their child will have earned the opportunity to be the Sheik's firstborn.

The Sheik thinks while they compete.

It was good to hear that voice again, an excellent memory to his youth, and learning the ways of tyranny. He is more skilled at it now.

Still glad he killed the voice's partner, he was weak dishonorable. How quickly he caved, how fast he told us all about his immediate mission, and then he lost his mind and started talking about being from the future. What camel dung that is.

A warrior in disgrace he had become. Having his body drawn to the four corners of the earth (or at least until the horses died from running through the desert at top speed) was the only way for him to regain balance in death and re-earn his entrance into the warrior's utopian kingdom. Even disgraced warriors deserve a chance at utopia. So the Sheik honored him with one more opportunity to earn entry.

Ten

Madelyne trains with her team; it is all they do these days. They have nothing else to occupy their time because none of the harem girls have tried escaping in a while, she wishes they would.

Unfortunately, Madelyne and her team are highly effective at what they do. Perhaps they should let one get away so that more will attempt to escape. It would take them a while to realize it was a "rare occurrence," then perhaps they would let another escape to encourage the process again. She scoffs at her brain's thoughts. There is no way she would allow someone to escape, perhaps kill them and leave them in the desert, then tell the others that she escaped...that is feasible.

Mostly Madelyne looks forward to a day when the sheik will let her go after men; she still resents that she is considered lesser and unable to hunt them down. She knows she can hunt anyone down. Kill them even.

Grateful that the sheik gave her a chance to do

something different, an opportunity to escape the harem. Even though she had risen to the top and was no longer eligible to be used by any of his men, she is still glad to no-longer be used as a sex object. There are plenty of others for that.

Madelyne instead, through her powers of persuasion and selection, ironically, planted a seed in the sheik that he needed women to go after the women that attempt to flee his harem. It is usually a new slave, or one that was beaten by one of the sheik's eviler men; unable to tell anyone that will do anything about it, they decide to take the risk and run off into the desert under cover of darkness.

The next morning, the captain of the guard, the meanest of them all, would go out with a search party. Each time he would report back that he was forced to kill the escapee. Eventually, the sheik discovered he was raping and murdering them, not even trying to bring them back to the sheik. Near impossible to prove, and also if he did, he could not punish one of his men for what his culture presents as an inferior species; instead, once he had proof, the seed Madelyne had planted sprouted in his brain and grew into fruition. He put her and some women of her choosing into an experimental training program teaching them hand to hand fighting, weaponry, and desert skills, including tracking. To this day, his men protest his progressive decision.

Because of this, he sometimes utilizes Madelyne and her team to humiliate men who have betrayed him, or the leaders of villages and nomads they raid. It is a tool to get that leader's people to succumb to his power. Humiliating their leaders somehow causes them to submit.

The most venomously opposed is the captain of the guard; he watches them from a distance. He growls unconsciously as he watches the women train. He would love to rape and murder them. If he could only convince the sheik that they betrayed him, then he could pound his will into them.

Eleven

As Gray sits and observes, he wonders how his team is doing. Deciding to check-in, he activates his comm.

"How's it going down there?"

After a minuscule, Miokel answers through the comms, "Good thus far. We are meandering the streets, at least on appearance. We are really tracking the path of each good as it is unloaded and carted off on the shoulders of the laborers and trying to casually follow it to its destination. There was enough of a couple things for us to follow to the end. I can show you those locations later. Nothing unusual to report at either of them, they are distribution points it seems."

"Great, thanks." Grey replies.

"Charles, how's it going with you and John?"

"Um, good Boss." Charles answers after a pause.

Grey smirks, "It cannot be that good if you are calling me boss. What did John do?"

"Well, he is still doing it. Attempting to pick up a woman, who happens to be a prostitute, that isn't really a woman but a man dressed as one."

"As entertaining as he is to you, now is not the time. Stop him and get him back on mission."

"Ok, Boss." Charles says, giggling.

Rosa and Mackenzie can't help but attract some attention. In a town with more than its share of seamen and at least a third of them liquored up, some would be sure to attempt some conversation even if they were not attractive. Usually, Rosa would put her game face on and scare them off. Yet, she knows Grey has Mackenzie and Rosa wandering together for a reason.

After far too many pleasantries and conversations, they came to realize the type of seamen that is attracted to smuggling only have three pickup lines: "Come help me with my mast.", "Is your Da' home?" or "How much?". Even though each sailor or laborer was patiently turned down, Mackenzie and Rosa were able to use their wiles to gain information. This they passed on to Grey when it was their turn.

"Rosa, how you two doing?" Grey asks.

"Well, you know. We've learned how to ask for sex in a multitude of languages..." Rosa says through the comms.

John interjects, "I will be needing that information later." he says.

"Other than that, we found out this stuff comes from everywhere, the ships converge here, are unloaded, then the goods are carried to various distribution centers. Most of it is then taken across the deserts with camels. Some of it is loaded up on ships again. They didn't really say where the ships go, just that they are loaded with an assortment of goods. That's about it so far." Rosa says.

"Good job, you two." Grey says.

Mackenzie pipes in, "All I did is stand here and look pretty. When do I get an auto translator? I want to interact, not just stand here!"

"After the probation period, Mac, which lasts for three missions, then is waiting for my report on you three, which is mostly done by the way. When we return, I will finish them that day and put in the requests for you three to have the surgery." Grey says.

"Great!" Mackenzie says.

"Oh, and I wouldn't say, standing there and looking pretty isn't doing anything." He adds.

"She's just jealous." Rosa ribs.

Laughter enters the comms.

* * *

As Miokel and June stroll along, they cannot help but draw some attention. She of pale skin and fiery hair, he of a local complexion and the presence of a noble, they attempt to look like he is taking his concubine on a walk around town. Perhaps while waiting for their ship to be unloaded. At one point, June adds to this image when she grabs Miokel by the arm.

Wrapping both hands around Miokel's bicep, she squeezes his arm to garner his attention. Feeling his arm stiffen, she rubs his bicep gently. "Playing the role." June says as she looks forward. People go back to their routines, Miokel relaxes his muscles and increases his saunter.

"So, tell me how you got to be where you are?" June asks.

"That is one hell of a question. Wow."

"Is it, why is that?"

He squirms in her arm a bit, although unwilling to let the strangers see his discomfort. Even June would have a hard time noticing if she wasn't holding on.

"I have forgotten my history."

"Forgotten your history! How does one do that?"

"With effort, that is how."

"We all have things we want to block out, honey, but

really... you cannot recall how you got to the trippers?"

"I know of my recruitment day, the moment they came up to me, not how I got to that museum or what I was running from. I know I was in hiding, I do not know why. If I did something or someone did something to me."

"Perhaps to your family?"

His muscles stay relaxed. "I don't think so."

"Perhaps you did something to someone else?"

Still relaxed.

"Or witnessed something."

Miokel's bicep twitches.

She continues, "Perhaps that is it. Perhaps you saw something and blocked it out."

His arm tight, he puts his hand on hers, squeezes gently and says, "Perhaps. This is not the time. We are working."

"Sorry, I did not know, was just making conversation. Better for me than worry. I feel out of place and obtrusive here, no blending for me at all. The people at the cafe are a testament to that."

"I can see that." Miokel says.

"You may have the opposite here, yet walking with me, you are an anomaly."

"Walking with you, I am the envy of every person who

sees us." Is his reply.

June's skin flushes, she smiles, and the lines leaves her face. The two walk back to the docks, having followed a load to its destination, they head back looking for more excuses to walk. It is an excellent day to be outdoors. The gentle Mediterranean breezes blend with the inshore desert air, creating a cooling effect, henceforth keeping the town an airy place to be. The midday sun beams down onto the village from above, cooking the adobe bricks even further. The insides dry as dust and the surface a glaze from the moisture. The smells of seaweed blends with baking bread, the sweat of laborers, with the scents of the mercantile's spices. There seems to be little worry on the faces of those in the town, a tiny sanctuary during a time of world strife. "What world war?" the town screams.

Charles approaches John, "I apologize for breaking up the fun, yet John, can I chat with you for a minute?"

Although both John and the prostitute are lost in their banter, the spell is broken by Charle's intrusion. Both express disappointment as John says, "Hold on, I will be right back."

He walks a few paces away with Charles. "What I was getting somewhere! Do we not have the time, because is there not always time to flirt, and getting information is what we are here for, isn't it?"

"Yes, it is. I just, I am not sure if you know that woman is really a man." Charles expresses sheepishly.

"Really... I have never been with one of those." John says and looks back over his shoulder at the prostitute standing there not so patiently, a look of frustration on their face.

Charles, without hesitation, "I am impressed and not surprised by your reaction. Yet, we are still working. So get to work. Information is what we are looking for. You have money in your pocket, use it."

John walks back to the prostitute, leans in, and whispers, "Can we go somewhere more private and communicate a bit?"

"Absolutely darling. Follow me." They saunter a few steps before turning into an alley.

Charles chooses not to follow, resisting the urge to caretake and blow the possibilities for John because of what happened last time John was in an alley. Instead, leaning his back against the adobe wall and raising one heel to the wall, he assumes a relaxed waiting position. Here Charles will stand until danger presents itself or John's exit from the alley happens. In the meantime, he might as well think about his girl, her sexiness, attentiveness, and understanding. Compassion being new to Charles, he is embracing it with earnest, albeit laced with bewilderment.

Charles is sure he is smiling when John departs the alley, the prostitute in tow. Both saunter with satisfaction. Nodding his head, Charles drops his foot to the packed earth, and, tipping his hat, he acknowledges the worker bee as he turns to walk with John and his ear to ear grin.

"I kinda want to know the details and kinda don't. So let us stick to the work stuff, for now, any pertinent information?" Charles' word use removes John from his elation trance.

John speaks, "Um, wow. And yes, gonna have to talk on it now, although I am not thinking too good, post..."

Charles' hand goes in the air. "Work stuff, John. Work stuff only." He says, laughing while putting his arm around the new tripper. They walk this way back towards their dwelling, enough work done for the day.

Twelve

Six of the tripper team stand in a circle for a short briefing.

"Where is Miokel?" June asks as soon as she notices they are one short.

"He left early. Wanted to get to the docks before they open for business." Grey answers.

"I thought we are off today?" John inquires.

"We are John. Do not worry. Miokel is doing his history thing."

"Didn't know he had a history thing. Hmmm." John replies.

"Will you walk to the bakery with me before you go off on your own?" June asks of John.

"Of course Mi Lady." Having said so, John mocks and already looking forward to their opportunity to walk and talk. A rare one since they graduated tripper school.

Rosa announces her day, "Mac and I are going for a

workout, outside of town. Do not worry. We will be aware."

"Ok, thanks for letting me know. See you at breakfast." Grey says, announcing a start time for tomorrow. Looking over at Charles, he says, "Speaking of breakfast, hungry? I'm heading there now."

"I am in. I'm craving some of that cafe coffee. Spoon standing it is."

Unceremoniously the team separates into many directions. All excited about the opportunity to play in a strange land. Tourist mode in full effect.

Grey and Charles sit in quiet peace. Having known each other a long time and both being of the strong, silent type, no conversation is necessary.

Charles takes a sip of the coffee, it arrived five minutes after the breakfast biscuits, and he wants to taste the flavor. He inhales through his lips and is rewarded; the coffee is thick, spicy, dark, and chewy. He savors its complexity, overwhelming the simple tastes of flour, butter, and yeast; he reaches for another biscuit and the butter.

A crash of pans and cutlery expands from the kitchen. Instead of a singularity, it crescendos. Charles knows breakfast is over. He reaches for the coffee as he stands, taking a big gulp as black robes burst from the kitchen area. Scimitars glisten in the window light as Grey and Charles freeze their motion when the front entry darkens as well. Within seconds they are surrounded by twelve mysterious figures, loose robes, and dust veils blending their details. The twelve rush the two trippers, ignoring blows, they subdue the two quickly and haul them through the kitchen out the open doorway to some waiting horses. Their captors throw them onto separate horses, hold them down tight and lash their feet and hands to each other under the horse's bellies.

Before either Charles or Grey can regain their composure, hands slap the two horses on their rumps and send them careening down the ally towards the outside of town. Into the desert, they run unabated.

With no required destinations other than the bakery, John and June ramble around the town. Two work friends on a day off while traveling for work.

"Did they have work trips in your time?" John asks when no one is in earshot.

"What do you mean?" June asks in return.

"Yah know, everyone traveling to Las Vegas to attend team building seminars or to Pittsburg for a supply chain management seminar, something like that."

June says, "I was not in that line of work."

John laughs. "I would think all lines of work would benefit from networking. You sure you didn't meet in bars or something like that?"

"We worked the bars, speakeasy, or wherever our marks socialize. So that would not suffice since we were often pretending to not know each other."

"We always had a hangout, a safe house. I guess that is where we networked, as you put it. Do you mean relaxing together, having a drink, playing lawn games, that kind of thing? Because once a grift started, we spent almost all of our time together. In the evenings drinking and games would sometimes occur. No traveling to a big city for anything, though, we avoided them because there is too much competition and experience in dealing with the evils of life. Usually, we searched for a town that had one lead meany and went after them. It was more effective and easier. I guess we were not as good as some."

John rebuts, "That or you were smarter than the average group. Left the competitive areas to others and sought out marks that were easier and perhaps with a higher success rate!" John's mind, semi-genius, if tested, seeks to find the win for his friend.

"What was America like in your time, John? Is it still America or like it is now? Based on what you and others have said, there are glassed cities, and that is it out there. That is different from what it was in my time. A lot different, back then, we breathed natural air, open windows, and screened-in porches to freshen the house and heat or cool it depending the season, if really cold the fireplace or dirty coal furnace. Some even had plumbing used to heat."

"You mean steam pipes? I have read about those." John asks.

"Yes, that, in the cities and factories, the rural areas not so much." June replies.

Their walk, a perfect stroll on a workday off, is suddenly interrupted by the sounds of pounding, the earth rumbles, and dust rises in the near distance.

"What..." John starts to speak.

"Horses." Is the only word to exit June's mouth.

John, without knowing, moves June and himself inside the nearest doorway. The midday shadows hiding them in plain sight.

Unknown to them, the two have wandered close to the cafe the team takes their meals at. A rush of black robe encased riders surround the area, a dozen or more dismount and enter or post up outside. Before any dust conforms to gravity, they all exit with the same calm haste. Streetside, it is unknown to the two that Grey and Charles are being roped to horses in an alley outback. It is not until they, along with the black-robed riders street side, watch a bunch of horses emerge from the alley that John and June see them strapped across horses. The baked goods John carries hit the ground and gather dirt as they roll away. John's eyes watch his team leader and new buddy Charles ride off into the desert. The dust of the multitude of riders in the midst of a hasty exit block his vision in short order.

Rosa and Mac, having run for quite a distance, are coming to a stop at an old structure. Abandoned and slowly being scraped from the desert's existence, the wooden corners are round and soft, grey with time in the sun yet still shade providing and enclosed on three sides. They step inside.

"That was a good one." Rosa pants through her breath.

Mackenzie smiles through her teeth as she catches her breath.

Suddenly the air fills with the sounds of hooves pounding the earth, thunderous, it echoes off the three sides of the structure. Both Rosa and Mackenzie put hands to face to protect their breath from the instant dust storm. Per their rider's command, horses lap around the outside of the structure, the pounding of hooves and volume of dust clouds the day.

Undercover of the dust and confusion, several black-clad figures enter and drag out Rosa and Mackenzie. They are dragged upwind and dropped on some sand away from the structure. Both are dusting themselves off and standing up when a woman standing before them thrusts out their hand and says, "Wait."

Mackenzie does not understand what the woman said; she does understand the hand gesture. Both Mackenzie and Rosa, one foot at a time, rise from their knees. Rosa speaks, "We are not subservient, you might as well know this now."

The woman in front of Rosa and Mackenzie and those surrounding them are dressed in a-typical horsemen garb, still flowing and dark to protect from the desert's heat and blowing sand, yet gathered at the wrists and ankle for mobility. All have their faces covered. Mackenzie and Rosa stand open-faced and defiant.

The numbers are horrible for the two trippers; surrounded by eight women, it will take a miracle to get out of this. Luckily Rosa might have what they need. First, to make some space.

"We prefer to take you unscathed."

"We prefer not to be taken." Mackenzie rebuts.

"Very well." The mystery woman says and nods her head once. Seven of the women surge inward to subdue.

Mackenzie moves outward and places a forward kick into the belly of the woman giving the commands. Air forced out of her lungs, the woman folds breasts to knees as she falls to the ground. The wind knocked out of her, she will be out of commission for a few moments.

Rosa removes her service pistol from its' hiding place within her tripper suit's specially designed pockets. She pulls the trigger twice before being overwhelmed with bodies. An angry growl, guttural, emits from Rosa, her Marine training kicks in, and she eliminates two of the attackers post haste. A quick change of their momentum has them lying on the ground with broken necks. Unfortunately for one, she did not die and will be watching the battle from a ground-up perspective.

Thirteen

After a rough ride strapped to horses, Grey and Charles are utilized as punching bags for a bit. They are then dragged in front of a tent, dropped onto their knees, and their headcovers are removed. The black-robed figures stand guard. Grey, bound and beaten, recognizes the man he is placed in front of, his brain flashes back to when He and one of his teammates were captured by a band of nomads on horseback.

Both Grey and his veteran ally were on foot, no match for well-bred Arabian horses. Having fled the scene of a mission gone awry, they were about a half-day walk from a walled city built to protect an oasis. The desert they were in consisted of what appeared to be never-ending sand dunes. The cream-colored sand blew about steadily, drastically changing the makeup of the dunes. The only constant being the slow relocation of the sand. One grain at a time, from one dune to another about a mile away, through this method, the sand leapfrogs its way to the only river flowing through the most arid of biomes. From there, it is carried to and mixed with the coastal waters. Then it is washed up by the high tides, so that upon the tides' recession each day, it can dry and be picked up by the winds to leapfrog the dunes once again.

Part of Grey was grateful when he saw the experienced desert riders appear in his already sand-filled vision. His first time in a desert, and he was done with it already. The rider's piercing eyes should have indicated what was to come, but he, then being the rookie, did not notice, instead hoped to be saved from a slow death by cooking in the sun. About twelve hours later, after an extended length of torture, he noticed.

Grey was forced to watch as his mentor, being tied to horses, accepted his random fate. The young desert warrior in charge had decided that Grey and his mentor were up to no good. That they are part of a group of seven strangers that had entered and then somehow escaped the city after trying to sabotage the only well in a 250-mile radius.

Grey watched as four men tied ropes to his mentor's wrists and ankles. The other end was handed to a desert warrior astride his horse. Both the horse and rider encased in all black. The flowing black robes and long black horse manes strewed about in the wind as the rider had wrapped the rope around the pommel of the saddle.

The young warrior had dismounted his horse and strode over to Grey, who was on his knees. He had grabbed Grey by the neck, forcing him to stand to watch his mentor being ripped apart by the strength of the horses.

Grey changes his focus, and the young rider transforms into the Sheik standing in front of him. He stands even on his feet, relaxed in known safety, more from his own skills than the nearby guards. Wearing luxurious reds and golds, he is adorned with the most exquisite cloth custom-tailored to his physique. Even though he is now apparently in charge, he still is physically active, perhaps still leading by action and marauding in deserts with his warriors.

The Sheik takes a step forward. He peers at Grey.

"It is you." The Sheik speaks in schooled English. The Sheik has always wondered what happened to the man after he released him all those years ago.

He looks deep into Grey, through his eyes and into his being, doing his best to find out what this man's life has been like. He seems older than he should be, well his face does, at least. The Sheik can see that the man is still active in life, but his beard and face show more wear and tear than the Sheik's. Perhaps he is less content with his life than the Sheik, and that worry ages him.

Grey looks defiantly at the Sheik. Well, perhaps that is the wrong way to put it. Confidence oozes from him. Not in an I dare you kind of a way, but a warrior before a warrior. It is just that at this moment, Grey happens to be the one bound tight at the wrists. Again.

"I recognize you as well." Grey says after a long pause.

After a moment longer, the Sheik says, "I apologize for your friend. It really was the right thing to do at the time. I would do it again if the same situation were to present itself. But I apologize just the same.

"I can see you also have been living as a warrior, a nomad traveler. What brings you here?"

Grey nods his head. They both know the other will kill as necessary. Grey opens his mouth to speak. The Sheik can't help himself; he lets a smirk escape the corner of his lips for a part of a second. Staring straight at his face, Grey notices.

"We are here on a mission, uh... .my apologies, what do I call you?" Grey asks, reaching.

"Don't bother with that." The Sheik says, emphasizing with a wave of his hand.

This sets even more of a tone for Grey. He chooses his words carefully. Not wanting to lie and not wanting to give away their mission, either he chooses a different tactic.

"I cannot tell you." Grey responds.

The man before him grins mischievously. "Since we have met before, let us cut to the chase then. I can tell by looking at you that you will not give. Will not tell me freely what I want to hear, yet will not lie to me either. It oozes from you. I honor that.

Instead, we will tie up your friend the same as the last one. You and I will fight. Whoever bests the other gets his wishes. If you refuse to fight, this friend (he points at Charles) will die like the last one. If you happen to best me, you will get your wish, I am assuming freedom will be what you wish. I could be wrong. If I win, you will tell me about your reason for being."

The Sheik makes a motion with his hand, commanding Charles to be tied up. A rope is knotted around each of his wrists and ankles. The wrist rope is tied to a pommel of a saddle filled mounted on a high strung horse. The black-clad rider keeps the horse prancing in place.

Wanting time to think, Grey says, "Sounds fun. I would love to leave my mark on you. I accept your challenge to fight."

The sheik smiles while motioning for Grey to be unbound. An unknown figure comes over and cuts the ropes binding Grey's arms together, leaving a cut behind. Grey licks the blood on his arm. And then, to dry the sweat off of his hands, grabs a handful of sand and rubs his hands together. Dropping the now damp sand, he picks up another handful. Having removed his outer robes, the Sheik turns and tosses them to one of his black-clad henchmen. He turns back towards Grey just in time to catch a bunch of sand to the face.

The moment the sand is in the air, and his palm is empty, Grey brings his hidden knife into said palm and leaps onto Charles. The look on Charles's face is something he will never forget, a cross between are you kidding me and gratitude. Grey is positive; there is a part of Charles that hopes Grey will kill him before these crazy bastards stretch his body until it rips into pieces.

No such luck.

Grey leaps astride Charles as if he is a saddle, reaches back, and cuts the rope attached to one of his legs. He repeats the process with the rope on his other leg. As Grey leans across his chest to cut the rope bindings around Charles' right wrist, the riders of the two remaining horse spring into action, spurring their horses. Charles feels his upper body lift out of the sand. He grips with all his might on the two remaining ropes with his hands. Charles futilely pulls on the ropes, fighting the strength of the two Arabian horses. By now, he has figured out what Grey is up to, and it is his intention to keep his upper body intact long enough for Grey to accomplish his task. Sinew and muscles rip as Charles yells to the heavens, he pulls in the strength of all warriors before and after him. Rage and power thrust from his lips, "AAAAHHHH!" he pulls the adrenaline into his body and wills his body to stay together.

Grey lunges for the right wrist as it pulls away from him. The war cry that Charles emits into the heavens gives him the strength to stay on top of Charles as his body bucks upwards off the ground...only have to touch the rope with its' razor honed edge. Almost...reaches. The horses pause to regroup, then as they surge one more time, the edge of the blade touches the rope and goes through it as if it were air.

The one remaining horse commanding Charles' body surges forward, free from whatever was pulling on it the Arabian charges for the desert. The rider, caught off guard, yanks on the reins in an attempt to stop the horse. He almost succeeds when unbeknownst to him, Grey does what he always vows is a last resort since you can only do it one during that particular altercation. He throws his knife. Grey performs this action before being conscious of his intentions. When Grey realizes the spinning knife will impact its intended target, Grey grabs onto Charles as if he were a long lost brother. Taking it a step further, he wraps his legs around Charles', their upper bodies firm against each other.

As the blade embeds itself into the horse's rear haunches, the horse launches itself forwards. Attempting to escape the pain, all instincts overtake the horse's training. It rears up, sending the rider backward and onto the ground. Free of his never-ending human burden, the horse launches itself forward, galloping as fast as possible into the vast desert.

The hot sand scrapes at the two as they career away from the Sheik and his men. The later's dumbfounded surprise still has them lacking pursuit. Or perhaps they figure the horse will finish them off.

Both Grey and Charles have this same thought as they hold onto each other for dear life. Grey cannot get to his backup knives in his boots, and Charles being the attachment point, is more ragdoll than anything else.

June stands tall, she beams with pride, somehow more radiant than usual, the sun, fire in her hair. Finally! Finally, she is not being rescued, used as a trap, or grifting someone. Instead, she is the rescuer.

Since the comms are working for once, she and John heard all the events that ensued after Charles' and Grey's capture. She and John quickly tracked the 14 horses to the camp, arriving just in time to witness the scene with Grey, Charles, and the sheik's men. Luckily, so enthralled by the day's entertainment, the sentries are shirking their duties and all instead, making sure they had a line of sight with the show. It is always fun for them to watch. Because of this, they missed John and June when they came riding over the dune and in line of sight with the camp.

Quickly turning tail and dismounting just on the other side of the ridge, June and John hobble their horses and crawl on the burning hot sand to the top of the dune, gaining a better view of the happenings below. Both become distraught at what they see. After a short banter about riding down and saving them, it is evident to the two rookies that it would be a suicidal action.

"We have to do something!" John exclaims.

"Like what, die with them?" June responds.

"I know. But...." He says

"There are like 30 armed men down there." She says.

"You could go down there and persuade them with your good looks." He retorts.

"You first." She responds.

John grins, despite the situation.

"Point taken." He says.

There is no way June and John could take on all 30 of

the armed, trained men located below. Feeling helpless, they also feel the morbid desire to watch the proceedings, at least to report to the superiors at home the details of Grey and Charles' demise. Although they both know the medical technology is superior in 2114, neither believe that the technology is advanced enough to reattach the ripped apart body parts of their teammates. They will inevitably be forced to gather when the black-robed men below have abandoned the body parts.

Luckily when Grey pulled his moves, they cheered, so the noise was lost in the chaos. They watch the men below start to chase after Grey and Charles when the laughing leader called them off. Unable to hear what he says to his men, they do hear his laughter.

June says to John, "We need to go. We have to stop that horse!" She backs down off the ridge and runs to her horse, skirts in hands. She leaps onto hers and spirits it into a full bore pursuit.

John, less enthusiastic about the horse, walks hurriedly towards his, still unsure why the horse lets him ride it and already sore from it, distracts himself by thinking of why he lets just about anyone that will, ride him. He loves the experience, learning what they know, or seeing the enthusiasm in their being. Perhaps that is what he thinks as he painfully mounts his horse, with minimal command, it surges to catch up to his buddy carrying June.

June rides in unison with the movement of her horse; once again, she is on her pony, the first one she had as a child. Everyone remembers their first, and for her, that pony was a saint. She rode the hell out of it, bareback and relentless, since the day it made the mistake of showing June that it could run. Maybe it figured it would scare this little child so it would run home crying to Dad and never bother her again. That was the plan in its mind, it backfired though. It was in that moment when the little redheaded girl first felt free from the constraints of childhood.

The very next time June was on the pony, she spent hours making the pony run, in circles, through the fields. Run, run, run. By the end of the week, June was Annie Oakley, she would make the pony run away from Indians, attack them, she set up rings along the fences and hanging from trees, she would ride full bore as close to the fences as the pony would allow and stretch for the rings as they sped by. About a week later, while at the Five & Dime, she spotted the perfect accompaniment to her play. It consisted of a holster for a cap-gun pistol, a two-toned plastic replica of a lever-action 30/30, a cowgirl hat, and a small red handkerchief. The first three times, June pulled the cap-gun trigger, the pony threw her. After that, it conceded to the noise. Or conceded to her rider's persistence. June had long since forgotten these memories, long ago filed in the archives.

Now, as she rides, nothing else exists. The earth turns in relation to her speed, she cries as she gallops her horse in pursuit of Charles and Grey. Thunder escapes the horse hooves as they push the earth beneath them, all is easy as the horse does what it was breed to do. June has picked a good one. She feels its breath, not panting from strain, but powerful in its love of moving fast, the horse is happy, not in a hurry.

As Grey holds on to Charles for dear life, he struggles to peak over his shoulder; he could let go of Charles and be just fine, but that isn't even an option, ditch one of his trippers...never!

What he sees when he gets a peek behind them implants in his mind forever. First, he notices fiery hair glowing in the sun, curly yet streaming behind its owner due to the speed she and the horse are moving. The horse, black as the light in an underground cave, glistens with sweat, the sweat flies upwards with each stride, June's skirts fan behind her as headgear, still worn around her neck in frustration streams behind her, translucent it gathers sand, sweat, and sun as it streams with speed.

He is not sure, but he thinks June is smiling. Grey smiles as well because she is gaining on them. They just have to endure for a few more minutes.

Grey closes his eyes and focuses. He thinks of nothing, freeing his mind from fear and worry about the outcome of his situation. Balancing out, Grey feels insurmountable strength, knowing he could hold on forever. He wonders about Charles, though.

The sound of repeating thunder is upon Grey before he knows it, he hears the thuds of the faster hooves slow to the pace of their tiring horse. Extra sand flies into Charles and Grey as June's horse comes alongside theirs and she reaches over to grab the reins, the horse actually slows before she reins it in. Perhaps it was looking for permission to stop before it keeled over and dies.

June pulls on the other horses' reins, stopping both horses, they naturally swing to the left. As they come to a stop, Grey and Charles' bodies roll to the right and come to a halt. June wants to dismount to help, but is unsure; she doesn't want the horse to move more than a minuscule inch. She looks back at two of the strongest human beings she has ever met. They lay covered in sand, Charles' arms are stretched to the max, he grips the rope even though he is unconscious, Grey's upper body is wrapped around Charles', his legs around the hips. Both are breathing, neither moving otherwise.

June calms the other horse, its nose is at full flare, its eyes are popping from its head, ears perked towards the sky. June's horse standing tall, wonders what is wrong with the other horse. This calms the freak in the exhausted one.

June dismounts and, moving slow, gives calming noises to the horse. She works her way to its leather bridle gets a firm grip while showing the horse some affection, something new to it. The horse instantly succumbs to her unbridled compassion. It is in horrible shape; she can see it will probably die. As bad as she feels for the horse, she is more concerned with the two people behind it.

The tow rope is long enough that she can turn the horse and move closer to where her idols lay, covered in blood glued sand.

As she approaches, she produces the same calming sounds she used on the horse, "It's ok, it's ok." Moving in, cautiously, she puts a hand on Grey.

He sighs.

He murmurs something...

June leans in close, "I'm sorry, hon, I didn't understand."

He tries again, "my boo..."

"One more time, hon, you are almost there." She says.

"In my boot..."

Keeping one hand on the reins of the two horses, she runs her hand down the side of Grey's body, maintaining contact as to not surprise him. Reaching his boot, she puts her hand inside and feels a knife. She never knew he carried a knife there. She learned about the one up his sleeve on her first mission with him. That was her first big eye-opener as to what her leader was capable of. She wonders how much she doesn't know about him.

June pulls out the knife. It must be in a sheath cause it comes out long and straight, what she would call a sticker, not the kind that you apply to books and windows, but the kind you stab inside of someone.

She uses it to saw the rope from the horse. Charles' arms fall to the ground with a thud.

Grey takes a deep breath and relaxes. His body falls away from Charles and blends into the desert's sands, his chest moves slow and deep. Still holding the reins, June settles in next to Charles, he is breathing slow and deep. She is unsure of what to do.

Alone.

She is rarely alone. She has always had protectors, her current protectors unconscious on the ground, she finds the roles reversed.

Charles' face is covered in sweat and sand, scraped with bruises to come. June unwraps the unruly headgear from her neck and uses it to clean around Charles' eyes, then his lips and nostrils. "Thank you, Angela."

June doesn't recognize the name. She doesn't respond. She just continues to clean his face best she can with a dry cloth. He begins to stir. She looks over at Grey and sees him looking up at the sky, trying to blink the sand out of his vision. Grey turns his head and looks at June, he smiles. She cries for him. His eyes glisten.

Still holding on to the horses, June works her way over to the salt-covered going-to-die-soon-horse. She removes the water skin from its secure storage and takes it back to Charles and Grey. Grey is sitting up, head hung between his bent knees, his arms resting on them.

Without warning, the horse dies, maybe its heart explodes, who knows, all June knows is it falls over, thrashes about for a few seconds, and exhales one last time. Relieved more than saddened, June lets go of that rein. She then looks back at the horse she was riding, and after making an eye contact agreement with it, she drops the reins to the ground.

Both hands free, she uses Grey's knife to cut off pieces of

her headpiece and pours some of the precious water onto them. Walking over to Grey and without saying anything, she hands him the damp cloth. Nodding his thanks, he uses it to remove the sand demons from his eyes. June kneels down and turns her attention to Charles. She cleans his face with the moistened cloth, he says, "Thank you." He didn't say that name this time. June files a question for later.

He is ok, she can tell just by looking at the color on his face. She applies some more water to the cloth. When she looks back at Charles, his eyes are open and looking at her.

"Your turn to save me." He says to her.

Her eyes glisten, flickering to hold back the tears, she nods to him, "You are my first."

Fourteen

Rosa and Mackenzie, fighting Madelyn and her crew, are widdling them down. Rosa finished off the last of the seven when Mackenzie chose to take on their leader.

Mackenzie is doing well-ish. She stands back up, removing herself from the ground, she wills the wild woman in her to the surface. A quick look of encouragement from Rosa is all she needed to step into the power that she already knows she has. Reminders are a good thing, particularly in moments like this.

Moving forward two steps, Mackenzie stops just outside of the stockier woman's reach. Being long-limbed isn't only beneficial when reaching a leg in to steal a ball from an opponent; it comes in handy during hand to hand combat. Knowing this, Madelyn strives to get inside her reach, where her shorter arms will have the advantage.

Rosa pauses to allow Mackenzie to feel her chops with

Madelyn. Rosa has been teaching the three rookies how to defend themselves as well as how to attack. Her personal martial arts training started on Parris Island, South Carolina. During her time of service, women were not allowed in direct combat, yet were taught the line-program, and later, Marine Corps Martial Arts. A compilation of all the quickest and most effective moves of any martial arts discipline the Marine Corps instructors could get their hands on.

The beauty of that type of training is it's filled with techniques where size is irrelevant to its effectiveness; it is all about the skills and mindset of the individual applying the methods. It is designed to excel in any type of environment. Right now, we will see how well Mackenzie's few months of training and her mindset do against an opponent from early in the twentieth century.

Rosa is excited to see what techniques this mad woman has. She has already seen her be brutal. Now Rosa wants to know if she is trained or a street fighter.

Madelyne makes another attempt to get inside her reach. Mackenzie feels this, circles, and side steps to keep her outside. At the moment-resisting the urge to box at her, Mackenzie instead looks for an opening in Madelyne's defense. Madelyne comes at her with a pugilistic style hand position, yet a martial arts style stance, Madalyne's flowing skirt with the tight cuffs lifts above her ankles when she assumes a horselike stance. This also lowers her body so that she is more underneath Mackenzie's defense than level with it.

Mackenzie, being trained by someone who is masterful in her fighting and small of stature, is used to the ability and desire to come in under a punch's path. Mackenzie throws a test jab at Madelyne, hoping she would choose to come in under it. Madelyne believing that openings should be utilized as soon as they are presented, did not fathom this lankier woman in front of her would-be setting her up. As soon as she ducks under the jab, she is met by Mackenzie's knee, rising into her chin.

Madalyn twists her neck slightly at the last minute. The knee that would've knocked her out careens off her chin and sends her to her knees instead of unconscious to the ground.

Mackenzie, in her newness, takes a step back to see what happens next. Next, she sees a handful of sand headed for her face and is forced to close her eyes for a second; it is in that moment that she feels a rush towards her.

Madelyne is surprised at her opponents' skills. This is why she is currently on her knees, underestimation at its finest. She will have to fight dirtier. On her knees, grabbing sand is quick and easy; she throws two handfuls at the woman face. As soon as the woman standing above her closes her eyes, she lunges up and forward, driving her forehead into the woman's soft spot, just above her groin. Not as soft as she expected, it creates a stinging pain to weave its way down her spine to the tailbone, her entire body shudders.

Although Madelyne's throwing of sand was a useful distraction technique, Mackenzie's level of fitness lessened the effectiveness of her follow up attack. It did cause Mackenzie to lose her grip on the surface of the earth.

As her feet leave the sand, Mackenzie feels herself bending over slightly as the head of the woman she is fighting drives into her lower abdomen. Mackenzie's many years of running and athletic training built strength in a commonly weak area of the human body. Although she leaves her feet, they quickly replant, and she decides to use her opponent's momentum against her. Mackenzie leans forward and wraps her arms around the woman's back at the waist level. Leaning back, Mackenzie lifts and falls back, intending to slam the woman to the ground.

Madelyne feels her opponent lean over her, and before she knows it, she is being forced over backward. There is nothing she can do but try to stick the landing. Doing the best she can, she manages to mostly get her feet under her just before she is butt slammed onto the ground. The superfluous momentum sends her flying forward and out of reach of the woman she is fighting, separating the two of them for the first time since they engaged.

Madelyne spins around to see what is going on behind her. She knows there are two of them and doesn't want them to take the opportunity to gain an advantage over her. It is in this momentary pause that she considers going for the knife hidden deep in her robes, too deep to gain a quick purchase, she will have to go with other things for now. She looks around her. They are in the middle of the desert, dunes are the only thing that surrounds them, the afternoon winds pick up, driving sand onto her exposed skin. It stings her. The sand reminds her it is the only weapon out here, other than what they brought with them.

Madelyne looks around, hoping to spot the horses. Although all of them are nearby, the reins are in the other woman's hands, the Spanish looking woman. Turning her attention back to the lanky white one she has been tangling with, she starts to lose hope. Her mind flashes back. She has had a long run, orphaned at six years old, she survived on the streets until her body gave her an out, surviving in the brothels from the age of thirteen to eighteen years of age, when she was forced to kill one of her customers in self-defense. Although it was self-defense, the man she worked for demanded restitution, for the man she killed was one of his advisors. If he had been family, she would've been killed. Instead, she became his to do with as he saw fit. The Sheik did not know what to do with her until she, once again, was caught defending her womanhood from one of his men. Although she was stopped before killing this one, her new role was apparent to the Sheik, who now owned her. He chose to use her in a capacity that would insult and create shame in men he was attempting to strong-arm or prove a point to. She was forced to whip men, pull them around by a neck rope, or any other form of public humiliation he came up with. In the 3rd time of using her in this capacity, he realized she enjoys the acts of humiliation, and her true passion in life was revealed: payback to the types of men that had caused her the most pain. Precisely the kind of snakes and weasels, he needed to humiliate the most to keep them under his control. They are the ones that needed constant reminding, their inherent nature to strong to resist temptations, even under his brutal rule.

Madelyne regains her feet slowly. As does Mackenzie. Both glance over to Rosa standing there, holding the horses' reins; both know she will not interfere unless she perceives Mackenzie is going to die.

This tells Madelyne she will have to kill Mackenzie quickly, allowing her to be ready when the Spanish woman takes action.

Mackenzie knows Rosa is allowing her to prove herself to herself. Mackenzie also knows she has a killer in her when needed, a warrior spirit that will kill what must be killed for others to live. Once again, that other is herself.

Both women move in for the kill; they swing at each other, manic passion in their swings, both attempting to apply a killing blow to the other with their fists. They stand there like two boxers toeing the line, exchanging blows, both trying to be the last one to apply the hit. After a few moments of this, Madelyne connects a blow to Mackenzie's chin with enough force that Mackenzie is forced to take a back step.

At this moment, Madelyne chooses to go for her knife, knowing that exchanging blows with this woman will not leave her much energy to take on the woman currently holding the horses. She is forced to kneel to the ground to gain access to the knife hidden within. She reaches and grabs the sheath with one hand to hold it in place while the other roams for robe free access to the blade's handle.

"Pick." Mackenzie says out loud, not wanting to risk misinterpretation in her brain. One part of her rookie gift from

Grey appears in her hand. Her will releases it from its' hiding place up her sleeve; it leaves the other parts of her lock picking kit behind and zips into Mackenzie's palm, with the pointed end extending beyond the hand's fingertips. Mackenzie grips it, steps forwards, and plunges the three-inch lock pick into the eye socket of the woman she is fighting. She feels it quickly sink through the soft eyeball and ricochet off the back of the eye socket, where it is directed by the eye sockets shape. The pick slides off the cartilage, plunging through the hole into the woman's brain.

Despite her inner warrior, Mackenzie pauses for a moment at the horror feeling of her hand touching the juice of someone's eyeball. The sounds of her lock-pick popping the eye, scraping down bone, and then squishing into the brain are half the cause of her pause. It reminded her of the only other time she had participated in someone's death, the squish of the brain reminiscent of her mind's memory of the sounds the trophy made when ending her husband's life.

Rosa standing there calm and patient as only someone of her experience can do, realizes when she hears the popping sound of the eyeball and watches Mackenzie's hand go into the other woman's eye socket, that the woman was done. Not knowing yet what Mackenzie had managed to get into her hand to make this happen, she is still totally relieved that it is over and without her having to step in and help Mackenzie finish her first fight to the death.

Mackenzie stands as stone. Her vision focused on her hand, her breath heavy from the fight. Adrenaline scourges her body, endorphins rise to the surface, she is on a game-high times two. Mackenzie removes her lock pick from the woman's eye socket and watches her fall to the ground. She flips on her side without ceremony. This is where she is sure to lie forever, sometimes covered by the sands, sometimes bleaching bones in the sun.

Mackenzie wonders why she doesn't feel bad for the dead woman. She tries to remember how she felt after she killed her husband. Right now, she feels the earth is better off without either of these people. Why be remorseful about that?

Fifteen

Charles and Grey, back on their feet, clean themselves up as best they can. Sand worked its way into every crease of their tripper suits and cracks of their bodies. They will have to wait for plentiful water before they can thoroughly clean everything. The tripper suits proved their toughness today, nothing like a long trip on sandpaper to grind anything down to nothing. Both men are in surprisingly good shape. Most wounds are isolated to the only exposed parts of their bodies, their heads and hands. The rest of their bodies were protected by the bombproof fabric and materials. An important note to make, both of their suits are still able to hold the hologram-like image of time appropriate apparel. Despite all the issues Grey's team has been having with the comms and auto AEDs, the suits' fabric passed muster, and accolades are in order. Not that that will ever happen.

The three team members sit in a circle, the remaining alive horse stands next to June. It is late afternoon and hot as hell. Both Charles and Grey have wrapped the pieces of cloth around their heads for protection, they helped June do the same. She still has yards of fabric left in her headpiece.

Grey speaks, "I think the best thing to do is to head back along our tracks before they disappear. If we get to a recognizable area, I will be able to navigate us."

"To where?" June asks.

"To where is a good question. We are scattered to the wind. Miokel is back in the seaport, probably wondering where the hell everybody is. Last I knew, Rosa and Mackenzie were on the run, who knows what their status is! And John, where's John?" Grey asks of June.

"He was behind me for a while on his horse, then he fell off. I looked back and saw him standing next to his horse, watching me ride away." June replies.

"So John is alone in the desert somewhere. Great." Grey says.

"Or he backtracked back to the encampment. I don't know what he would do when he got there. Although maybe he could navigate back to town." June says.

"Unlikely." Charles speaks for the first time. "Very unlikely, he has no outdoor survival skills, he isn't trained in navigation, with or without devices. He is from a time when that wasn't necessary. I'm sure they had something implanted in them or in their food pills to help them find the toilet. So John is probably done." Charles says.

June glares at him, "You don't know that! John is a survivor, he may be an idiot, but he isn't stupid. He will figure out something."

Charles nods his head, he agrees he isn't giving John the benefit of any possibilities. He needn't remind himself of what is survivable, plus why mess with June's head right now. "I think we grab some of that horse meat and start walking back, following the horse prints and drag marks, till we can no longer find them or figure out something else to do. That has to be better than sitting here, baking in the sun."

"Agreed." Grey says.

They all look at each other and nod.

June is on her feet in an instant, "You two lead, I will follow with this horse. We can strap on anything we need from the other horse onto this one." To her surprise, both Charles and Grey are still working their way to their respective feet, moving like they have been dragged for miles through the desert by a horse.

Leaving the heavy saddle on the dead horse, they acquire the reins and all other easily accessible leather straps.

There is no food to be found. Yet a scimitar and a smaller dagger are added to their cargo. As well as a skin filled with tea—a blessing.

They carve out a few chunks of the horse's flanks, wrap it best they can in some more material and place it inside one of the saddlebags on June's horse.

Now up and moving, the two battered men move at a firmer pace. Both will feel their ride for days, or at least until they get back to medical, where pain meds and miracle solutions will be implemented. First, they have a walk ahead of them. The three move off into the desert in a single file, following an easy trail and wondering how far this trail will remain visible.

John, hating the whole horse thing, walks the same trail, albeit in June's original direction. He walks slow, his horse beside him. John attempts to use the horse as shade, but the sun is firm in the sky, preventing such luxury. For some reason, he was able to figure out the headpiece with ease. It looks comfortable on his head. He wears it mostly closed, with a slit just enough apart to allow his vision. He looks out ahead until the trail disappears in the distance and wonders how far it goes, determined to follow it to the end. The wind blows hotter than the air; it strives to remove the moisture from his body. John's body is all covered up; its task is errant. His fear level rises as he notices the trail he is following getting fainter in the dune reorganizing wind. Its daily task eternal.

John fears he will wander here until he dies.

He stumbles.

"Get it together, John!" He scolds himself.

He allows himself to pause for a second and then takes another step, and another, and another. He focuses on his feet for a few steps, making sure they are moving again. He brings his vision back up to the horizon and sees a black dot off in the distance. He keeps walking.

After about 30 more steps, the dot becomes four dots, one larger than the others. After many more steps, he recognizes the dots as humans and a horse. The waves of heat prevent him from identifying the figures, yet he knows who they are.

John makes a beeline for them.

Sixteen

Miokel practices invisible. He wants to blend in as someone of this time, pretending he is from a town on a different shore of the Mediterranean Sea. He also wants to watch the regular activities of the area. If there is a stranger in the midst, it may change things.

Miokel hangs in the shadow of the docks. He's been here for most of the day, long enough to get a good idea of the ebb and flow. This is his choice of activities on his down day.

Having a down day while on mission is extremely rare; he thinks this is only the fourth time in all his missions. It does make sense somehow. The team had a quick task, probably a clean-up mission, something the computers picked up after the team's return to 2114 that needed to be fixed or tweaked. Perhaps it was something he and the rest of the tripper team did that left an undesired impression on the past, so they had to fix it, and coincidently there is something a couple of days later that needs to be handled. How about we save a billion dollars or so and have you all stay an extra day. Ok? Cool.

After watching and observing, Miokel knows at least eight other people are doing the same. A couple he thinks are out for their personal interest, wanting to get their hands on some of the smuggled goods or remove the profits from someone else's pockets if that seems more their style. A couple of the others are in charge or looking out for someone else's personal interests. They watch certain items and ships with an eagle eye, while totally ignoring others.

He has noticed all of the others watching the day's activities keenly, from time to time, go down a certain small alley. There are a multitude of avenues and pathways on the docks, yet they all go down the same alleyway. Miokel knows he has to obtain access to that alley; the person he is looking for will be found there.

Whenever there are humans and the activities that go along with them, there is a cacophony of sound present. When one finds themselves alone in the woods, there is a thunderous silence. The tinnitus rings in the ears, the wind is a roaring river, the insects are boisterous, and the birds their own melodic version of white noise. As Miokel takes in the sounds and activities, an unsounded signal brings all the humans to rest. He must have been lost in thoughts because his ears picked up the change first. The sounds switched from men talking, boxes sliding, and the laborers' footsteps to seagulls speaking their delight, gentle waves kissing the pier's legs, and the sounds of the shore breeze finding the buildings' cracks and crevices.

Miokel glances around and, after a moment, spots what he was hoping for. A few of the men in charge, the watchers, gather around a square crate, settling themselves on barrels and getting ready to play a game. He waits a moment longer. Miokel smiles; he knows the game.

Miokel saunters over, the man facing glances at him and then looks back down to the game, having filed Miokel as a non-threat to his game.

Although Miokel has and is practicing his native language, he is grateful for his translation chip; he is a tad nervous about entering into a relaxed banter with the locals. There is no way the systems developed in 2114 could have taken into account the local dialect variables of 1917's southeastern Mediterranean. A complex blend of Turkish, Persian, and Arabic. No matter, he approaches with confidence, knowing that he would detect irrational fear if it was coming at him from a stranger, he gives the benefit of the doubt to these men as well. They are alive and in charge, after all. While everybody else quickly eats their lunches, these five men settle in for a relaxing game of Okey.

Miokel thanks the Geeks as he speaks into his translator. "Greetings, I see you are playing Okey. My father loved this game. It was the first real game he taught me, as he used to like to remind me every time we played.

I wonder if I might join in?"

Three of the men glance up at him. None of them speak. After a moment or two more of uncomfortable silence, the man with his back to Miokel and everything for that matter, takes his turn. Unable to play tiles, he fishes around a bowl until his fingers find the one that feels right. After adding the numbered tile to his others, he turns to look at Miokel, sizing him up.

Miokel does the same at a glance. What he sees is a man of Permian and Asian mixed descent. A handsome blend of both nationalities. He is also clean, as are the others around the table. It is one thing not to be dirty from the absence of physical labor; it is another thing to be clean in the year 1917. Sure there is a big sea to jump into, or baths in the town, or other ways to get yourself and your clothes washed, but these men have clean nails! A stout difference.

It is the man's friendly eyes that Miokel notices next, kind and bright they beam at him, no hatred for his intrusion.

Instead, they are filled with curiosity.

"Of course. Why would I disallow you the constant reminder of your father? It would be dishonorable for me." He replies.

"Thank you, I am grateful for the opportunity, he was a great man." Miokel grabs a barrel from the pile nearby. It smells like gunpowder, for danger and intrigue reasons, an interesting thing to rest his laurels on. He is sure this barrel brings a high value in this time of war. Gunpowder is being expelled by the tons each day and night in the trenches of Europe. No matter which side of the war this gunpowder comes from, it will be missed.

"Thank you, your hospitality is appreciated. Might I return your kindness a bit by sharing these black grapes I purchased from a child around the corner a short while ago?" Miokel says.

One of the men smirks. He knows the children around the docks work for the same person they work for. He distributes the produce to them every morning and receives the income every evening. It is also his job to punish those that skim from the monies earned, this part he relishes a little too much. Probably why he was given the job. His prowess ensures the boss can stay hidden away in the back of the alley, protected from the noise of both the streets and the docks, he lives his years away in the paradise he has created. His every desire and luxury delivered straight to him as it arrives from the docks, the best of the treasures going his way first, instead of towards the big house on the hill. His version of treasures, at least.

The top man at the table speaks to Miokel as they restart the game, "What brings you to our docks today? We have seen you watching and observing."

As it comes to him, Miokel takes his turn, placing a matched set of sequentially numbered tiles down in the play area. He tags on a 12 and a 1 tile to some tiles already in play. Then answers the question with truth and some adornment, "I wandered into this area looking for work. Once here, I noticed this is the type of active shore town I was hoping for, and the docks are where it all begins and ends. This is where the power and wealth transfers. I want some of it. The money more than the power, I have no need to be in charge. I am content somewhere in the middle, as long as I get fresh sea air and money to pay someone to clean my clothes, and myself for that matter."

The men around the table chuckle, for they have these luxuries. Not all are content, though. At least two of them covet the top man's position and his boss' position, the ultimate goal being the house on the hill. The same place, Grey and Rosa acquired the jewels and rocks one tram ride ago.

The man introduces himself after a bit and asks the same of Miokel, "I am Jaques, spelled J-a-q-u-e-s, pronounced like the children's game."

"Miokel is my given name." Miokel says in reply.

"Where are you from My-O-Kel?" Jaques asks.

I am from an inland town called Crossway. We children growing up there called it Crossway of Nothing.

"How is it you love the smells of the seas, when you are from an area such as that?" Jaques asks.

Miokel thinks of the stale air he is forced to breathe when he is down in their top-secret underground bunker. Although piped in from the canyon's pine and cedar scented breezes, by the time it reaches his nostrils is contaminated with the smells of the pipes, metal ductwork, and other manmade stenches. The best smelling air while underground is drawn into his lungs when he is standing on his balcony. There is a unique blend of the rock's earthy metallic scent mixed with the fresh foods made for the workers; those smells waft up naturally from the Commons a few floors below. To Miokel, the distance and blending with the rock's essence keep the food smells from being too overwhelming.

Miokel answers Jaques, "It is because I am from the Crossway of Nothing that I love the intriguing mix of scents coming to the shores. Crossway just smelled stale, nothing new coming or going. The crossroads are so remote and outdated that there is nothing to smell."

"Why are there a crossroads there then?" Jaques asks.

"...Because of the Romans." Miokel responds.

Jaques nods, that was the thought in his head.

"I don't know. Well, I know it was a supply route for the Romans when they were attempting to expand their empire. Once that area no longer needed the insurgence of supplies, the Romans stopped coming, and the road grew silent. Because of the dryness of the area, even the few wagons that come through every month will keep the road passable forever." Miokel says, managing to catch himself before speaking a lie, as keyed in on honor as this man is, he might detect lies with ease. Miokel will have to be careful.

While engaged in small talk, Miokel and the others crank out three-games of Okey. For those that did not grow up in the area, Okey is a game of strategy played with tiles hosting different colored numbers. The goal is to match color runs, sequential numbers of the same color, and runs on the same number. A simple game that gets exciting with creative minds playing.

Towards the end of their fifth game, the noise around them shifts from seabirds and waves to the bustle of human productivity.

"We have to get back to work, boss." One of the players says to Jaques. He nods his head and, with a hand motion, agrees. The four men stand and with nods and a "good to meet you." Or two, they head back to their duties.

Jaques says to Miokel, "Before you get up. Let us go meet the boss, I think he will like you. Interested?"

Without pause, Miokel nods his head, "I am interested. Thank you."

Jaques stands, and Miokel does the same, "We will check on a few things, then I will take you." Jaques says.

Without further comment, Miokel follows and grins at the opportunity to get an inside view. Then he gets to walk the alley and meet his personal mission for the day.

Miokel and his new friend saunter into the alley, the buildings on both sides are tall, straight, and windowless. Once beyond the entrance, the only light that enters the alley space is from the sky two stories above them.

Miokel is always great at presenting a stoic outside

demeanor, sometimes while freaking out on the inside. This is not one of those times. Based on the day's conversations, he does not have to worry about this boss doing anything irrational. He always makes logical moves and decisions, per Jaques, that is.

They walk to the end of this section of the alleyway and turn left as it forces them to do so. At the end of the alley, another 20 yards or so, stands a solid wood door with three goons lounging around it. Goons are defined as "big, burly, humans whose job it is to pat-down or pummel people as required." They always seem to love the pummeling part and resent the pat-down. Miokel is hoping to avoid a pat-down. He isn't carrying anything he doesn't want them to find; he just doesn't want them to find out his clothes are not what they seem to be. He is hoping any pat-down is lite at best.

He needn't worry, although all three come to their feet as they approach the end of the alley, a simple hand gesture from Jaques has them side-stepping. It appears he has the authority to skip pat-downs.

Jaques knocks on the door and a peek hole opens. Two eyes appear and disappear as the slide is moved back into place, a click is heard through the door, and then it opens. The heavy door swings inwards, revealing a large entryway lit by torchlight. As they both step inside, Miokel understands the lack of pat-down. There are ten men in the room, all are highly armed and bored. It seems there is little need for their rifles and scimitars, although each carries both. The place is furnished with ornate wooden benches and tables, all sorts of exotic items are strewn about on the side tables. The two tables in the center of the room are adorned with fancy drink cups and a large assortment of foods gathered from many locals. A few different pastimes are there as well. There is even one goon cleaning his rifle and eating cherries simultaneously. Life is good in this room.

"Wait here." Jaques says as he walks towards the far corner of the room and disappears down a hall.

Miokel nods and says his greetings to the men in the room, a few reply, and all go back to whatever it is they were doing. None seemed threatened by his presence. He decides to walk over and see what type of rifle the man at the table is cleaning. The fact that he is even cleaning it says a lot. As Miokel gets to the table, there is a whistle from down the hall.

Without looking up, the man cleaning the rifle says, "He will see you now."

Miokel nods his head and, knowing that the worse first impression would be to keep him waiting, walks towards the corner hallway. Walking down the hall, he feels the healthy body tension created in situations like this. If he didn't carry fear, he would be crazy. The key is to keep walking through the fear.

After a few steps, the hallway turns right and opens into a larger room. The room is full of audacious items; even the five women in the room are audacious. This boss is into excess or collecting, or maybe it is the prestige that comes from having exotic impossible to get items from around the world.

"Look at what I have done." Is the first sentence out of the under-boss' mouth.

No, it's the feeling of power he is into.

Duly noted.

Miokel takes a detailed look around the room, it is what the under-boss wants, so it makes it ok to do so. Otherwise, it might be considered rude.

What he sees impresses him. Gold and jewels are in different forms everywhere, the naturalist form being of gold bricks and rough-cut gemstones. They can also be found in any creative arrangement you can imagine, jewelry, plates, armor, and in ancient forms as well, probably from Egypt, Roman Empire...you name it.

His stomach rumbles as it senses the next section of the room, it is filled with spices, a giant wooden table loaded with herbs and spices so precious they are in the tiniest of jars. In contrast, although valuable, others are plentiful enough to fill up sacks pilled under and around the table.

Miokel's eyes rest briefly on the weapons section of the room. He barely notices the audacious ceremonial junk for the impressive collection of some of histories best weapons. Someone here knows their stuff!

One of the reasons he was brief on the weapons section is that at the same time, out of the corner of his eye, his brain registered his greatest passion, history!

He wasn't able to hide his body's truth responses when he saw the piles of scrolls and books. He was a kid in a candy store! Ancient scrolls containing solutions to the mysteries of his brain's wonder. Heavy leather books with giant latches and locks, rigid tubes with old greek writing adorning the outsides of them. Miokel takes an involuntary step towards them and then regains his bearing, steps back, and turns towards the under-boss.

"Impressive, very impressive." Miokel says.

"Yes, and you gave away your weakness, your Achilles heel. Did you notice?" He asks.

Flushing slightly with embarrassment, Miokel responds, "I did."

"So much so, that you did not even look at my women. Do you not like women?"

"I do." Miokel responds.

The testing begins.

"Then why do you not look?"

"I did not want to be rude."

"I appreciate that." The underboss turns and looks over at Jaques. He says nothing; he simply nods. Jaques sits down and relaxes.

"Have no fear Mr. Mickel."

"Miokel, sir." He corrects and tests back.

"Thank you, Mr. Miokel. You may call me Sir Edacity" After no reaction from Miokel, he continues, "It is amazing the power of a name, isn't it? Is it fate, could my parents have known or did I become my name?" he asks.

Miokel replies, "Great philosophical questions. I love to philosophize and think. As you noticed, I am into knowledge, particularly historical knowledge. I like to learn how people used to think and what they used to believe..."

"You more than like." Sir Edacity interrupts.

Miokel nods in acknowledgment, giving him the win as desired.

"Yes, I do." Miokel answers.

The man stands and walks over to Miokel, the women in the room tense, not from fear, from preparedness.

"You just figured something out, didn't you, Mr.

Miokel." he says.

"I did." Miokel says.

The man nods and puts his hand out, granting him permission to speak it. Commanding it.

"Your biggest passion is not women either; they are here as deceptive protectors. Although you are into men, they are not it either. No specific item or object is your biggest passion. Your biggest passion is possessing things you cannot have." Miokel says.

"Aren't supposed to have." He corrects Miokel.

"I can get my hands on anything, I can force my will on anyone, I can kill to take anything I want, either using my own hands or theirs." He waves his hands, implicating the others in the room.

He looks at Miokel, wanting him to figure it out.

"Your biggest passion is getting others to hand over their prized possessions...willingly."

The man smiles, big and genuine.

"Yes, Yes, YES." He says. He puts a hand on Miokel's upper arm, besides squeezing and testing his bicep, he also escorts him over to a table to sit down.

"You are correct, Miokel. For example, I know you will never hand your sexual body over to me willingly. There is no way I could persuade you to do so. Therefore it is of no passion to me. Even if you are a fine example of a human being." He says, grinning. He then lets go of Miokel's arm.

"Please sit." He invites Miokel to his table.

Sir Edacity turns around slightly, and one of the females steps forward, "Would you like some tea." She asks.

"I would." Miokel nods and replies.

"It is good to have your people cross-trained to fulfill many roles. It keeps your costs down and allows you to treat them better. Then they will stay and, more importantly, be loyal."

"Are you the loyal type?" he asks Miokel.

Miokel feels a tinge of guilt.

"I am." he says.

"What are you loyal to?"

Miokel laughs.

He knows he has to speak his truth, this has the feeling of a final test.

"The greater good, my version of it." Miokel says.

"Aah, excellent. The last part is an important part of the full truth." The tea arrives as Sir Edacity says, "This is going to be a good afternoon. Now we just have to figure out a fair trade. What you can provide me, so that I can grant you access to the information you desire."

"Let me be honest, I can tell you will not be here long term." He turns and looks at Jaques. "You did good, but he is not a long-termer, still a great find. You may go back outside and resume running the place. I will give you your finders fee and evening bonus. It will be worth it." Sir Edacity says.

The man stands, Miokel does as well. "Perhaps a rematch?" Jaques asks.

Miokel smiles and nods, "Perhaps."

As he walks out, Miokel sits back in his seat. The woman, finished preparing the tea, leans over and sets a delicate teacup in front of her boss. She then comes over to Miokel and leans in to place his; she brushes her breasts against him as she does so. Startled from the unexpected, he glances at her, she makes full eye contact with him. Miokel sees her beauty, Persian, as is he, and intelligent. She is here because she wants to be, not a slave. It seems Sir Edacity was not kidding. You have to want to give him your prized possessions.

It is not often Miokel gets to be around others of Persian blood. There just doesn't seem to be any others in the tripper program. He feels a part of him awakening, fear in his belly, a hardening a little lower, and a desire to talk with this woman while lying in bed, sweat drying, and breath recovering from passionate sex. Miokel sees fear and desire in her eyes as well. This might be a great day.

Miokel nods and thanks her for the tea as she stands. The woman gently puts a hand on his shoulder, pauses for a moment saying nothing, and then walks away.

"She wants you. You can be with her, but first, let us talk." Sir Edacity says.

Miokel lifts the teacup to his lips, thin and dainty it has taken on the heat of the contents, he is forced to hold it by the delicate handle only, thumb and forefinger squeeze together while he tips the contents onto his lips. Hot, spicy, fresh, home...are the thoughts that cross his mind. Interesting.

"Ok, let's talk." Miokel says.

Miokel walks back toward their local home-base. It has been a great long day. He capped it off with a few more Okey games with Jaques, a perfect ending to an unexpectedly perfect down day. He and Miokel came out even after a couple more games, they chose this. They could have played one more, but why does it matter? They both are excellent.

His thoughts wander to that intelligent Persian woman he also got to spend a few hours with. He never asked her name, she never offered it.

As soon as they were in a room alone together, the passions rose to the surface. Within seconds they were kissing, wrapping tongues, and pausing only to exchange longing looks and remove clothes. A minute after walking into the room, they are standing naked, both bodies rising in temperature as they embrace, explore, and entice each other's lust.

Miokel cannot remember the last time he got to be with someone of the same bronze skin tone as he. He revisits the encounter as he walks.

His eyes, typically closed during sexual encounters, are open, and he draws them across her skin at every local, her shoulders, her round breasts, darker nipples. He runs his hands down her front, from her forehead to her nose, then chin. The back of his first two fingers press light as they run down her upper chest, through the valley between her breasts and onto her firm belly. Sweat glistens, appearing instantly with his touch. She kisses him deeper still. He moves his hand to her rump and squeezes, she pushes her body against him. She wants him inside.

Running her hands down his arms, she brings him over to her bed and helps him lay there on his back. She massages his entire body, starting at the tip of his toes. She works his feet, knowing every spot to touch and massage, then upwards to his calves. She works her fingertips deep into the muscles of his thighs and running her hands up across his belly and onto his chest, she straddles him. She puts him inside her as she, one at a time, massages his hands, takes time on each finger and the palm, and then works those magic fingers into his forearms, stretching and pulling the muscles gently, working out all the knots.

There is no reason for her to move her body as she sits on him. He is aroused by the care she is giving him. And the view, the view as he watches her work is astounding. Her hair, black and wavy, long on her shoulders and chest, glisten in the candlelight. Her full breasts, high on her chest, thrust out to be seen through the long locks. She is attentive to her work as Miokel watches her, her eyes on her hands' placement and area of work.

He reaches up, gently wrapping his fingers on her neck behind her head. He also seeks out a specific spot where the neck and skull connect, full of nerves and power. He works his fingers into there and pulls her down towards his face. He kisses her with thankfulness. She puts her hands on his chest and pushes away strong and gentle. "Almost." she says, "One more." Keeping him inside her, she repositions backward a couple of inches, drawing him to the hilt, she helps him set up. She also wants to work his head. She works her fingers into his scalp, slowly down through his think hair, the fingertips find his skull. Once there, she traces them through his hair, to massage on all parts of his skull. Her skills are astounding.

He feels her dripping down onto him. She loves this as much as he.

Her massage done, she pulls his head towards her chest and holds him there gently, not forcefully, as she squeezes him with her muscles, she orgasms, powerful and quiet. Then she smiles when she feels him do the same.

He couldn't help it, as he remembers. He wanted to last forever, to thrust into each other for hours, yet it was impossible. Powerful.

He remembers the greatness of lying there with her for what seemed like forever afterward, although it was probably less than an hour. Yet, it was a lifetime of utopia.

They talked minimally, both having things to hide. They shared the one great gift they could give each other, their bodies. Their energies intertwined, knowing they were meant to do so, and when complete, they both got up, dressed, hugged, and after intense eye contact, went their separate ways, knowing it was all they could have.

Miokel sighs out-loud, gaining a strange look from a couple of drunk sailors. It reminds him he is no longer in her safe embrace. Instead, he is out in the world again—time to put his metaphorical mask back on.

Seventeen

Miokel, while emitting a soft whistle, saunters into the walled section of their Kangal dog guarded space behind the humble adobe house. When he spots the rest of the team consuming beverages in a sitting semi-circle, his whistle stops. The entire team is encased in the desert sands, two-thirds of them are also covered in bruises and cuts. The worst damage to John and June appears to be some sun damage.

Miokel says, "You guys obviously have a different definition of a down day than I do."

The team pauses in shock.

Instant scowls fade and meld into laughter, soft and quiet at first, the team then takes the opportunity to release the pressure of the day. One day back in time that will change many things for a couple hundred years to come.

After some much-needed laughter, Grey rallies up the team.

"Ok, we don't have time to get as clean as Miokel got himself today, but we do have time to freshen a bit before grabbing some food, and then we have to hustle back to say goodbye to the dog and catch the tram-ride home." He says, looking at his wrist.

Grey goes to put his arm around Miokel. Miokel steps back, laughing, "No, no, you don't, not until you are at least half as clean as I feel right now."

"Would I be right in saying you are cleaned out in many ways? You have this glow about you." Grey asks, already knowing.

"Yes, it was a good day, an actual down day. Should I be worried about the day you all had? It seems I was left out of this mission." Miokel remarks.

Grey replies, "I am not sure, but we will find out soon. Perhaps we will be back here again to accomplish the mission you and I had laid out. Or perhaps this was the mission, and maybe we were set up to think differently. There is something amiss. I can feel it. There are too many things going wonky on our missions."

Miokel nods his head in agreement. Both he and Grey are long term trippers; they know the ebb and flow of the technology. How long it takes their bodies to recover based on the differential between their present-day and mission date. Both have had missions go right and go wrong, and to tell the truth, nothing gratuitous has really gone wrong in the past. Strange right? No, not really. With the program's technology, it is a surprise that anything goes wrong.

"I agree. The comm's not working properly, two AED failures in three missions instead of the historical once or twice a year..."

Grey interrupts, "And today. Today it seemed this sheik, whom I will be telling you about later, knew exactly where we were and what we were doing. How is that possible?"

Rosa, who had been eavesdropping, chimes in, "And the thing, incident with John in Namazinga-2."

Both look at her inquisitively.

"John got jumped while puking in an alley. That's not something that has ever happened before, and not something that regularly happens in the city period. "Utopia by design" seems to be working. At least by what we see during our visits and from talking to our bartender friend there. He has no problems with violence nor knows of any in the city. The population numbers are maintained meticulously at the proper levels..."

"What do you mean by 'proper levels.'" Grey asks.

Charles jumps the conversation, "Proper ecological levels."

Miokel and Grey, knowing he is into this type of stuff, wait for him to continue. The rest of the team is attentive and smirking.

"I learned in my night school Ecology 101 course, that the higher the density of any living thing, the higher the rate of disease and violence. This is true in plants and animals, including humans."

"This is based both on scientific studies and experiments." Charles says.

"What's the difference?" June asks.

"The difference is, in the studies, the scientists look at real-life environments and collect data based on what they observe and measure. In experiments, they set up a situation to prove or disprove a theory. This always includes a "control," meaning one thing is kept natural or given a placebo. For example, fake items that influence nothing more than the mind of the animal or a plant treated precisely the same as it would be in its natural environment." Charles answers.

"The point is, it is only when the animals or plants get desperate that the violence kicks in, or times of excess that the disease kicks in. Excess is a high density of food for the diseases, bugs, viruses to feed off of. They appear when excess is prevalent."

Grey is slowly shaking his head.

"What?" Rosa asks him.

"I am marveling at the pastimes and knowledge that you all have." He replies.

"So, what you are articulating is, based on years of science and research, that the cities are maintained at population levels designed to eliminate competition?" Miokel asks.

"At least for resources, yes." Charles replies.

"There is still the human factor, though." June speaks, "The human factor is a wildcard. Just look at how I survived before I came into the tripper program! Grifting is simply using a human's natural tendencies against them. People see me, my demeanor. I smile to tell them everything is ok, and because they want to believe what their mind is telling them, we grifters can get what they want from them."

"Even if part of them knows it is happening?" Miokel asks.

"Yes, even though part of them knows the truth, they want to believe you are a good person, even if you are not. It is why we were able to take advantage of them. " June says, looking remorseful.

"The opposite is true also." Rosa adds. "After years of military and police service, I didn't really trust anyone. It seemed everybody I came into contact with had something to hide, when it turns out, only the types of humans I was dealing with had something to hide. Good did still exist, it just wasn't part of my natural world."

"In fact, it wasn't until Charles and I starting going to Namazinga-2 to play that I was reminded of a peaceful existence. I am grateful that I am reminded of good people, peace, and other awesome things like that." Rosa adds, glad that she has moved on from her many years of regular violence. Swat teams only deal with the worst days of a human's existence, those that are held hostage or holding a gun to their own heads, people that have gone so far off of the deep end that shooting them dead is often the solution. Before that, the Marines, well Marines are shock troops and wedge makers sent into turmoil areas to create or end situations. At least that is her perception of who she is.

Grey, although non-participatory in the conversation, is taking it all in. He is allowing it plus his existing knowledge to percolate in his mind. He knows it is not a coincidence that he ran into the sheik that killed his early teammate. It is not a coincidence that the AED's failed, or any of the other things. None of it is a coincidence or just happening. It is the "human factor" statement that helped it all click.

Who and why are the big questions to be answered. It could be the new Colonel, although Grey doubts it. He is squared away and brought in to advance the program. Grey knows this to be accurate; his instincts tell him so. He lets his brain run through random names and people he knows from the facility. None of them really rise to the surface as a viable suspect except one, "Hahaha!" He laughs and shakes his head. They are so obvious, he missed it.

Grey's team looks at him when he laughs, waiting for an explanation. He gives none. Looking at his arm again, he knows they have to get moving. Grey uses his left arm and hand to create the universal let us get going signal as he squelches that voice in the pit of his stomach that tells him otherwise. Grey makes a mental note to talk with Miokel before their down days. He wants to run the thought by him as well. The weasel Grey is thinking of might just be able to pull it off.

Eighteen

A man strolls up to the outside of a nondescript structure on the edge of town. Nonchalant enough that when he bends down and flicks open a lighter, lights it, and applies the flame to a pile of straw, no-one notices. He pauses for a moment more, ensuring the straw is burning as desired.

Satisfied, he stands up and walks away, a "click" can be heard as he closes the lighter. His hand then seems to disappear inside his beige robe and removes itself a moment later, sans lighter. Behind him, the flames lick upwards, the full sun currently hiding the fire, it will go unnoticed until the black smoke develops, by then it will be too late.

All standing in their ready positions, the team prepares to launch. Charles stands defiant, bruised and battered, steam oozes from his pores. Part of him smiles at how they were rescued from that situation. He looks forward to laughing and joking about it with the others as soon as they return. Not home yet, he holds onto his hope.

Mackenzie rubs her knuckles; many parts of her are sore already, so that is not why. She stands there, feeling her power. Rosa's lessons are sinking in, Mackenzie is becoming a badass, has always been one she realizes now, never one to be a victim, she now has the fortitude to do something about it. She wonders if she can go back and beat her husband's ass before he cheated on her so much, then maybe she wouldn't carry the guilt of killing him.

John grew up and spent most of his life in an era of customized health. All food was synthetic, everything was artificial. Alcohol and tobacco were no longer produced from natural ingredients; instead, one could pay to have them added to their pills or purchase black-market pills. He had never tasted alcohol, or smoke, until his recruitment. This might be why he smelled it first.

John standing there doing his, I'm not going to die mantra, he started saying it in his mind since his first tram-ride ended in him being zapped back to life by Charles. He is taken from his focused thoughts by a strange smell, somehow he instinctually knows what it is. Opening his eyes, he looks up and sees a dusty grey floating in the air, it's wafting through the opening between the top of the earthen wall and the thatched roof. Using the air currents, it twirls its way in joyfully. John is resisting a voice in his head as he watches the strange aberration fills the upper regions of the rafters. It isn't until he notices the same smoke coming from under the door of the next room that the word whispers from his lips, "Smoke." then his brain clicks into action, "fire, FIRE, FIRE, FIRE!" John can't help but yell the words. As he does, the realization hits him, and he defecates in his pants a little.

Like the other rookies, he is positioned in the middle of the formation, and John feels all eyes on him.

Grey turns to look at John, first with a look of what-the-fuck, that quickly changes when he sees the smoke filling the room.

Grey stands ready and waiting. He hasn't had to keep time for years, yet he wonders if his timing is off for once. He thinks they are late; they are never late.

It is at this point that John starts yelling behind him. Fire? What is he talking about? He better not be messing around! Grey turns to look and sees the room filling with smoke. He makes eye contact with Miokel, who's eyes are wide open; he mouths one word to Grey, "When?"

Grey looks at his invisible watch out of habit, buying him thinking time; they are late, and he knows it. "Everybody out!

Let's go...move, move, move!" Grey says. Still professional in his urgency, he moves toward the door motioning everyone into action. Miokel, standing in the back, pushes everyone towards the door as they reluctantly start moving. All are tired and just want to go home. They aren't up for this bullshit!

Grey reaches the door, lifts the latch, and pushes it open hard. He is looking back into the room, waving his people forwards with his hand, wanting to propel them out the door faster.

A loud concussion works its way into the room through the door, streams of clean air force their way towards the team. Grey's body reacts as if its been hit by a moving train. His feet, head, and arms fold forwards as a shotgun blast bends his body in half. The middle half heading for the back of the room, the rest of his body trying catching up. Grey flies backward at hyper-speed, red mist and flesh expand from his body the instant the pellets hit his torso, the rookies behind him are sprayed with his essence, he flies unassisted until his body hits June. June, who was moving towards the door as her boss commanded, thoroughly confused, but taking action anyway, is floored when his body collides with her forward motion.

Seven figures enter the building at a rapid rate. Pre-stacked for entry, they are inside within a second. All are armed, their shotguns and automatic weapons pointed at the confused team.

Rosa and Charles are the first to go for their weapons, expecting this, three of the people entering the building have the barrels of their weapons inches from their faces before they can unholster. Proactively one of them applies a rifle butt to Charles's temple, dropping him to the floor.

Not a word is spoken.

Tension and smoke lay heavy in the air.

Miokel walks forward, a shotgun is pointed at him at close range. He doesn't stop his forward motion; he is stepping up to one of the individuals. He knows them.

Miokel keeps his hands open and facing forward, with his arms down at his sides. He doesn't want to get shot. Yet, this is important. He walks up to the only female in the group of people that just entered the room. She sees him coming and prepares herself. Miokel works his way face to face with the woman, they stand with faces inches apart and their toes almost touching. She is dark of skin with long black hair pulled back and tied with a piece of leather. Adorned in warrior clothes appropriate with the time frame.

Miokel stands tall. She holds the same height and meets him eye to eye. Defiant in her gaze.

"So, this is the path you have chosen." Miokel says to her.

Her eyes flair, her lips twitch. She stands unbudging.

"Enough." The man with the smoking shotgun says.

Miokel stands there, the woman obeys the command and turns away. Another steps before Miokel, training their weapon on him. Two feet apart, both know a pull of the trigger would send five or six rounds into Miokel before anyone could blink.

The seven strangers own the room, the one with the still-smoking gun wastes no more time and moves over to where Grey lay on the ground. June has managed to get her torso out from underneath Grey and sits with her legs trapped. She could finish pulling her way out; instead, she sits transfixed on the man with the shotgun. He stares at her with stone eyes, dead to emotion. She watches him come over; he keeps the shotgun barrel pointed at her absentmindedly.

June, although new, gives it a thought. She looks at his hand holding the shotgun, she sees his finger lightly on the trigger, while the rest of that hand grips the gun with a firm hand. Trying something would be her death.

The man squats down, maintaining eye contact and his blank look. When he is sure she is a non-hazard, he turns his attention to Grey. Reaching through the hole in Grey's tripper suit, he feels around inside. Finding what he is looking for, he grasps it in his hand and pulls out a bloody hand.

June can see a robust woven steel rope running from the man's hand to Grey's neck.

Having no choice, the man rests his shotgun on Grey's chest. Although he knows she is not a threat, he leaves it pointing at June anyway. He leans forward and uses both hands to remove the wire from about Grey's limp head, letting the head fall back to the ground. As he pulls the cord towards himself and puts it around his neck, June sees a crystal, or piece of glass, something...hanging from the wire. She is straining for a better look as it disappears into the man's clothing.

Without further ado, he retrieves the shotgun, stands, and turns for the door. No words are spoken as the seven, cautiously, work their way back through the door. By this time, the room is engulfed in smoke. The heat is rising, and flames are licking under the door from the next room. It is only a matter of moments before the fire will work their way through the barrier.

The moment the last perpetrator is outside the threshold, Rosa rushes the door, a heavy woody sound is heard from the outside as the door is barred shut. Rosa's shoulder hits the door, it doesn't budge. They are trapped.

Nineteen

Miokel, still in the back of, what is left of their tram-ride formation, observes the occasion.

Grey lay on the ground before him. Bloody and non-moving, his condition is unknown. Charles also non-moving, probably fine, just unconscious. Rosa leans against the barred door, panting. The three rookies are kneeled around Grey, staring at him.

The only thing taking action in the room is the smoke as it strives to fill the space. Come to think of it, the fire, doing its damnedest to turn the other entry door into charcoal, is taking action as well.

All humans are non-moving.

Brains bring the strangest thoughts, in the most unusual moments. The instant Miokel's realizes what he is about to do, the thought, Well, so much for being number two, flies through his brain and runs for the tongue, almost as fast as the rest of

Miokel's body springs into action. Something else comes out instead.

"ROSA! Take my position. John help me pull Charles over to the center of the room. Mac, June, stop that fucking bleeding!" Miokel says, pointing at Grey's chest.

The smoke's pathways change as the team springs into action, billowing anger just the same. Rosa keeps her vision on the ground as she moves around to Miokel's usual position in their travel formation. She hears him and John drag Charles into the middle of the formation. Stepping with purpose, she puts her left foot in the boot impression Miokel left in the sand. The imprints he left were as if he literally sprang into action. Balls of the feet deep in the sand left pushed back imprints, while the heels barely show. When Rosa steps her right foot into Miokel's print, then and only then, does she bring her eyes up. What she sees is imprinted on her vision forever. Her long time pal and her boss, both prone on the ground, the newbies circled around them. June moves to hold Charles' hand, she puts her head on his chest. Perhaps to listen for his heart. Rosa then looks up at Miokel, he looks back. His eyes are haunted and prevalent with fear—confidence preservers through as he turns away.

She watches him step into Grey's position, glad he did. She isn't ready to be in charge of a team again.

Rosa focuses on the back of Miokel's head, trying to will the process to begin. Whether she influenced it or not, the smoke starts to swirl, dust rises from the ground, intermingling. No papers fly about, just plenty of sand and smoke. It threatens to resurface all, including the trippers, as the Einstein hole appears to whisk the tripper team of seven, more or less, back home.

Except it didn't.

Miokel's brain is confused, not only because it is used to seeing the back of everybody's heads upon arrival, but also because his mind thought it was going to see the wall in the underground facility. Instead, it sees old wooden walls, dust, years of it, tools pilled in corners, old hay bales, and a hole in the wall leading to the outside, it thinks based on the smells coming in through it.

Fresh air. Not processed.

Miokel's brain forgot about the double jump and the layover in the heat of the moment.

He stands there, unmoving.

Life is brutal at times. Like, when everything is flowing great, easy-peasy as they say, then without warning, you are thrown a colossal curveball. The one your biggest fears told you was going to happen someday, and you've spent too much time worrying about it, even though you knew the chances of it happening were a bazillion to one.

The team stands, statues all as the atmosphere in the old storage shed recovers from the time-travel energy. The electricity releases its hold on the soil, bits of old straw, and dried skin from whatever it is that lives under the forgotten hay bales, in the back of this forgotten tool shed, in a forgotten area of a vast country. The team is oblivious as to where and when they are.

Tension, the tension in the air, strives to bring the electricity back, strives to break everything, crush it with the weight of its fear, heavy, tangible, and terrifying.

As the dust finally settles, we see Rosa standing in the number two spot in the back of the formation. What she sees is most of the team on the ground before her. And a great unknown standing still at the front of the formation. She knows Miokel has what it takes to lead a team, she also knows he doesn't desire to do so. She may have to step up.

Miokel breaths in the dust, his body taste tests it, attempting to confirm what it knows to be true. They are not back in the safety of their underground facility. There is no medical team racing to save Grey, and possibly Charles. They have arrived at their mid-jump layover point.

Miokel zones in on the wall and breaths some more; it seems like hours, albeit only a second or two. It is the sound of crying behind him that springs him into action.

He turns around to see what is going on behind him. The crying is coming from Mackenzie, and he didn't expect that. She isn't crying over Charles as his instincts are telling him. Not even Grey, laying there pale and dead. She has a hand on an unmoving June. Except for when Mackenzie crescendoes up to a sob, then June's body shakes with her.

The wicked thought, "I'd better move before Rosa falls over dead also!" Flies through Miokel's brain as he springs into action.

"Rosa! Help me!" he exclaims. "Get the spare AED from Charles and use it on June."

Rosa leaps from her position and lands near Charles, feet first, then falling to her knees and sliding to a stop into his rib cage. Knowing exactly where he keeps his AED, she reaches through the illusion his Tripper suit provides, into a deep pocket, located in the lower back region, and yanks out the tiny device. Without looking, she tosses the device to Miokel, who catches it. Rosa then puts an ear to Charles' chest.

Miokel catches the AED with one hand, "Mackenzie,

lookout." He says.

She does nothing, continuing to sob.

"Move!" he yells at her.

He reaches up and slaps her. Hard. Her hand goes to her cheek on instinct, leaving its place on June's rib cage. Miokel pushes the go button on the AED. There is no slow countdown or computer voice to talk him through the process, just electricity taking over June's body. Her body tries to bend itself in half as the charge surges through her electrical system. To its ends and back, the current flows. A second time. Nothing.

Miokel hits the charge button for the third and final time. He is told that if they don't revive after three hits of electricity, to "move-on," whatever that means.

He pushes the button sending the current. Then waits.

"I'll do it." Mackenzie says, regaining some sense of composure. She could put her hand on June's chest or two fingers to that pulse always found on the side of the neck. Instead, she leans over and puts her ear to June's chest. She wants the last opportunity to connect with her, sending some oxytocin with her touch. "Boomp, boomp thud, boomp, boomp thud," is the sound she hears coming from June's chest cavity.

Miokel looks on intently, not sure if it worked. He is confident he will give Charle's AED a run for its money if June's heart is not yet beating. He will probably keep doing it until the never-ending battery ends. When Mackenzie sits up and looks at him, he knows all is okay. For that look of despair is gone, and a glimmer of hope is in her eyes. Not much enough to give him his answer, though.

Miokel wills his eyes away from Mackenzie and forces his vision to where Rosa kneels next to Charles. She nods her head to him and says, "He is breathing. Probably has a concussion though, another one that is. I'm not sure how many this is for him." Miokel nods his head, knowing he is okay. For the first time, he looks for John; he hasn't noticed him as of yet. His vision finds John sitting on the hay bales, head in his lap, hands pressing on his temples.

Miokel speaks, "John." He looks up. "I need you to do something for me. Go see if that vehicle is stashed in the barn, we are gonna need it." He looks over at Rosa next, "You better clear the outside real quick, then on watch."

She nods and heads for the human-door located in one of the giant sliding doors. The memories of the first time she cleared this area flash through her senses, the sound of the bumblebees bumbling, the rotting apples fermenting, that gratuitous fresh air. This time she exits the shack with her favorite weapon in her right hand. Her 1911 is loaded and ready to go. In fact, such is her sense of caution today that she thumbs the hammer back as she exits the door. Pure business is her attitude as she listens, looks, and stalks around the building at a rapid rate. Knowing quickly, all is clear in the immediate area. Good thing too, cause when she rounds the final corner, she sees John running as fast as he can towards the shed where they stashed the Zuk van.

She watches him move, graceful as a gazelle with tortoise legs. His shape is changing. Now that he is active, he is losing that jello shape that humans take on when they eat too many carbs and sit still all day long. In his case, for a generation or two.

He hides it well; Rosa can tell he is flabbergasted. That is one thing she is coming to admire about this rookie. He gives a damn. He does his best, and is no-holds-barred, who he is, and he is okay with it.

Taking her focus off of John, she pays attention to the rest of her surroundings. Sweaty as she is, the cool breezes give her chills. This time, however, it is strangely warm and humid. She feels a static in the air as well. It is about to storm. The lack of breeze tells her it is soon to come.

Twenty

Colonel Petzer waits for the team's return. He stands at the bottom of the stairs that leads to the tram-ride platform. The technician Loren, informed him that being any closer would be "bad," not seeing any need to inquire further, he waits there. Being in-charge has its privileges. It has taught him to ask for what he wants, even to the extreme. It often pays off, just like him getting to experience a Tripper team returning from a mission.

Before he has the time to get lost in thought, he feels the hairs on his arm standing up, then the coarser hairs on the back of his neck, even his high-reg military hair cut stands a bit taller. In front of him, little swirls begin to form on the platform as dust particles and then papers scrape the platform's surface before turning into mini dust devils and rising for the ceiling. This wind creates out of nowhere and then Colonel Petzer sees the lights. They look like orbs or what the child in him thinks of as fairy lights. They dance with delight at the work they are doing, prancing a bit before becoming part of a swirling pattern, counterclockwise as his grandparents used to say. Having watched four departures and the same in returns from the looking window above, he knows this is a return based on the energy swirl pattern, clockwise for departure into time and counterclockwise for a return to departure time. He confirms his thoughts with this, his fifth return.

Colonel Petzer stands tall, cracks his neck left and right, and just in case, puts his hand on his sidearm. A sleek looking pistol made of old school materials and modern technology holds 25 rounds per cartridge. He is a qualified expert through a program he helped develop. The instructors didn't give him any slack, either. Proud of them, he is.

When the team suddenly embodies the room, an energy force rocks him on his heels. He knows per Loren's instruction, he still has to wait until the energy dissipates or he may screw something up. Again, enough information for Colonel Petzer to watch and wait for the dust swirls and papers to return to the surface.

He counts to ensure there are six team members left and that Grey is elsewhere. Having the ability to do so, Colonel Petzer chose to have Grey sent direct. He stands, his hand on his sidearm and watches the energy swirl, looks deep into the space between now and then, hoping someone was dumb enough to jump through. They weren't.

When the papers hit the floor, Colonel Petzer removes his hand from the sidearm and gains the steps. "You are safe. It's ok." He says to them as they turn to look at him. Rosa and Miokel take a step towards him. He sees them think about reaching for their weapons and realize they aren't there. Just in case, Colonel Petzer had all items removed and they will be waiting for them in their respective apartments.

"I am Colonel Petzer, newly in charge and angry as hell. Let's get you patched up, fed, and then we will regroup to address this head-on." His audacity and straightforwardness seem to have done the trick; he sees the team relax into their exhaustion. "First, those of you who are not, on your feet. Let us get off this platform."

He watches the team ease into action, all on the verge of shock and exhaustion they move towards the stairs and him. He descends the stairs with ease, walks a few more paces, and then waits. When they get to the bottom of the stairs, he walks through the swinging doors with them slightly faster than their speed, and they all pass through the trap doors and biometric scanners. Through the other doors and out into the hall, he walks with the team, a swagger in his step. Well, swagger is the wrong word. Purpose. He isn't feeling cocky. He is leading one of his teams, a team that lost one of their own, their leader. He has to put a new one in place for the duration of the walk back to the team's meeting room that is him.

When he gets to their ready room, he opens the door and holds it for them. "Please grab some food, water, sit if you want, then we will debrief." He says to the team as they enter. He watches each as they walk by him, the bubbly redhead stares straight ahead, Rosa, the former Marine, wears her stone face, the geeky weird dude smiles at him and nods, Charles rubs his head and says nothing. Miokel is second to last, his eyes are squinting and deep in thought. The former soccer star comes; next, she is carrying a swagger and fighting scars.

Colonel Petzer pulls the door closed behind him, the rush of air heard in the quiet hallway, tugging it until the latch clicks shut. He gets himself some food and water. Knowing from experience that the team will be reluctant to eat, he leads by example. Then in a hushed field voice, he speaks.

"I know it was a rough one and that Grey's status is DOA. That is about it. Catch me up..."

"We were ambushed, sir." Rosa says.

"It's fubar." John says, using one of his new words.

Miokel speaks next, "It is another tripper team, Colonel, or at least they used to be. I recognize... their training. Seven of them just like us, armed, wearing tripper suits. Pre-planned. They started a distraction fire, not only did they shoot Grey on sight, but they also took something from around his neck."

Colonel Petzer nods, "What else? Any details about the Trippers?"

They all speak simultaneously, Colonel Petzer puts his palm up in the universal, that is enough sign. "That is a yes, I will have each of you sit with a sketch artist. Also, a written debrief so I can read them all. I know we are a paperless, off-book operation, yet this time I need to be able to digest and read the same version repeatedly. It is just how I think." He finishes.

"In the meantime and to be militarily brutal, in the realms of the king is dead, long live the king. Miokel..." Colonel Petzer walks up to Miokel and thrusts out his hand. Miokel takes it. "You are the team leader. We will get you a seventh team member when this is all sorted out. In the meantime, I am working with you all."

Colonel Petzer finishes with, "Congratulations, Miokel."

"I take things like this serious, not just losing one of our own, but how it happened. Internal sabotage is the worst kind of betrayal and will be dealt with swiftly and with intention." They unclasp hands as Colonel Petzer takes a step back. "Condolences on your and our loss, Grey will be missed."

"Now, I will let you all get to your food. I bet you are famished." Without hesitation, he heads for the door and with haste exits the room. Once outside, he picks right and heads down the hallway until coming to a corner, he rounds it and pauses, back to the wall. Whew, that still sucks, he thinks to himself and puts his head in his hand.

Twenty One

Mr. Roberts walks into her office, on-time as expected.

Sitting behind her grandiose desk, made of local stone and a 500-year-old slab of Alligator Bark Juniper, the desk owns the room. She, a tiny figure behind it, is accentuated because there are no other contents in the 800 hundred square foot room. Three walls stand stark and tall, seeming to be made of a ground-up-basalt-rock mixed into concrete, the floor a red-stained concrete. The fourth wall is all windows. Said windows look across the tops of all buildings between it and the enclosed edge of the city. Beyond its clear impregnable protection, the tracks stretch east from the city, with a blur racing towards a far shield volcano across the valley.

Mr. Roberts is snapped back to her presence when she speaks, the impatience and disdain reminding him who's office he just walked into. "Well?"

"It is done. Mission accomplished, my dark-haired

maiden." As he says, this Mr. Roberts gets lost in the blue sheen of her hair, the darkness of a new moon night.

The scraping of an unseen chair changes his focus. He salivates as the woman moves, slowly, with two fingers of each hand firm on the desk, she rises to her full height. Four inches taller than Mr. Roberts, she has a great view of his perfect hair. The same darkness as hers, its added sheen produced by hair product. She rides her eyes down his body. Working from the hair, down his face, to his impeccably tailored 1980's power suit; she knows he cannot walk about the city wearing it, not even the upper levels, so she knows he changed his clothes in the receiving room's bathroom, and yet he still looks perfect. Once she reaches the shoes, she is thoroughly aroused. But he doesn't get to know that he must not think she is so easy.

She releases the pressure off each hand, the color returning to her fingers as she removes them from the desk. Maintaining eye contact with Mr. Roberts and moving at half speed, she reaches below the juniper desktop's back edge and pulls open a hidden drawer. The entire desk is made with experienced hands, the stonework performed by seasoned masons, and the juniper slab harvested and worked by perfectionist carpenters; thus, the drawer hardly makes a sound.

The room is so silent, its' tinnitus rings.

The drawer whispers as she slides it open; his breath quickens, she controls hers. He notices, and his breath increases more.

A smirk escapes her bearing a millisecond before she catches it and puts her discipline back in order. The sound of the drawer reaching the stopper on the back of the drawer ends the game. Maintaining eye contact, she reaches in and withdraws two, four by four-inch padded blocks and a piece of cloth. Still looking at Mr. Roberts, she sets the two pieces of padding into the center of the fabric and, grabbing opposing corners, she brings them to the middle and ties them into a bow. She does the same with the remaining two edges of the fabric. The woman then glides her way from behind the desk and makes her way to where Mr. Roberts is standing.

He watches the way she moves, sinister is how she moves her body, its as if a snake were standing on the back third of its length and using it to propel itself forwards. He loves watching her hips when she does this, it is where the movement stops. The bottom and top half of her body blend the movement and non-movement there. The pear-shape of her hips are magic.

The woman throws the package at Mr. Robert's chest, he catches it with both hands as she says, "I will finish you, then you will bend to my will for the rest of the day. When darkness comes and I am satisfied, you may go."

As he bends down to do his task, she adds, stern and parental, "You better not have any plans."

He unwraps the package, on task, so perfect in his motions, that in a matter of unhurried seconds, the towel is laid flat before him, and each of the padded blocks he made for her are placed at the precise location she requires. This accomplished, he stands gracefully.

She moves over to stand in front of him, just off of the towel, she stares at him intently, and waits till he averts his eyes downward, then and only then, does she lower herself to her knees.

Mr. Roberts waits till she is engaged and busy before he allows himself to relax into it. This works because she has not realized that he knows she needs this as much as he does.

He smiles, sinister, mischievous, twisted.

Hours later, he walks into the empty hallway from her reception area. Thoroughly exhausted and simultaneously elated, he thinks about their success. They supremely buggered up the chancellor's plans; at least, according to the woman, he just spent the evening pleasuring. They make a hell of a team, she and he. His experience in the spy world and her involvement in the political world makes them a power team.

Mr. Roberts loves the adrenaline rush he gets from working with her and playing with her, knowing it is only a matter of time before he kills her.

Afterward

I am elated to release book three of The Tripper Series! This manuscript was first worked on in 2017 and sat for three years due to life changes and other book releases demanding my attention. While roughing out this manuscript, about 10,000 words of book four were written simultaneously. Neither was touched for three years.

2020 has provided me an opportunity to finish this manuscript and the first of three in my thrilogy. Here Be Dragons also gets to be released in 2020. The best part about releasing both of these is I get to work on the next manuscripts in both these series—two entirely different formats, purposes, and training grounds for the author that is C.M. Halstead. The short form of The Tripper Series provides practice in keeping an audience engaged through quick, aggressive storytelling, the goal of a complete hero's journey in about 40,000 words. The longer format of the "dragons" series is practice for me to incorporate the hero's journey in a longer, epic type format, several cycles in a three-act, 120,000-130,000 word story. This may be as wordy of a book, that my attention span will allow me to write.

Each book of The Tripper Series encompasses a different theme, a parable of sorts. Not to tell tales of religious growth, to tell tales of personal development, stepping through fears to get what you want, relying on a team, allowing oneself to be a hero, and good stuff like that. All while encased in a sci-fi format designed for quick reading, escapism, and fun.

I find book three, Seasons leaving me aghast, and I thrive on what comes next in the series. Book four, Everything Changes, is next. The midpoint of the seven-book series and the long hero's journey that the entire set contains. There are seven books and eight-plus cycles. What is next? Roves around my brain as I go about my daily tasks.

More works By C.M. Halstead

<u>The Tripper Series</u>: Trip Walk and Kangal are the first two books in this adventure, time-travel series. In Trip Walk, we are introduced to a team of seven "Trippers." Trippers are the special forces of their time, so new that no-one knows they exist, they are time-travelers by trade. Kangal, book two of the series, gives us a little more insight and another opportunity for the rookies to gain experience. Book three has us returning to "the scene of the crime," and the tripper team finds out that something is not as it seems.

<u>Mongers</u>: Inspired by events in modern America, this was intended to be a 5,000-word short story and blossomed. Reviewed as "prophetic" and "spot-on," 'Mongers' is a unique heroes journey.

<u>The Tracker</u>: is my first released story. It is a refreshing satire